S0-BIQ-736

CRITICAL ACCLAIM FOR STEVE BROWN'S *SUSAN CHASE MYSTERIES*

"It's a rare man who can write from a woman's point of view and make it work, but Steve Brown succeeds beautifully!"

—**Gwen Hunter**,
author of *Betrayal*

"A distinctive voice, tough-on-the-outside, tender-on-the-inside female."

—**Christine T. Jorgensen**,
author of the "Stella the Stargazer" series

"Setting and plot make this an entertaining winner. Highly recommended."

—**Katy Munger**,
author of the "Casey Jones" mystery series

"It's fun to read a book that is not in the least like the ones you write, and at the same time is a snappy read."

—**Elizabeth Daniels Squire**
author of the "Peaches Dann" series

ALSO BY STEVE BROWN
published by ibooks, inc.:

<u>SUSAN CHASE MYSTERIES</u>
Color Her Dead
Color Me Gone
Color Me Guilty
[coming May 2004]

COLOR ME GONE

A SUSAN CHASE MYSTERY

STEVE BROWN

ibooks
new york
www.ibooks.net

DISTRIBUTED BY SIMON & SCHUSTER, INC.

For Peter O'Donnell

A Publication of ibooks, inc.

Copyright © 2000 by Steve Brown
Originally published under the title
Stripped to Kill

Although cities, locations, and organizations mentioned in this book
are real, any references to them, and all characters and events, are
for the purpose of entertainment only and are part of
a fictional account.

An ibooks, inc. Book

All rights reserved, including the right to reproduce this book
or portions thereof in any form whatsoever.
Distributed by Simon & Schuster, Inc.
1230 Avenue of the Americas, New York, NY 10020

ibooks, inc.
24 West 25th Street
New York, NY 10010

The ibooks World Wide Web Site Address is:
http://www.ibooks.net

The Chick Springs Publishing World Wide Web Site Address is:
http://www.chicksprings.com

ISBN 0-7434-7997-1
First ibooks, inc. printing February 2004
10 9 8 7 6 5 4 3 2 1

Printed in the U.S.A.

Acknowledgments

I would like to thank Mark Brown, Phil Bunch, Missy Johnson, and Bill Jenkins; Cathy Wiggins and Lesta Sue Hardee of the Chapin Memorial Library for their fact checking; and my favorite Generation Xer, Stacey, for making me sound slightly hip, and, of course, Mary Ella.

1

I have to admit I had no idea someone as simple-minded as Nancy Noel could doom my relationship with my new boyfriend. One of the last times I saw Nancy, she was still at it—dooming my relationship, that is. She was sitting on a curb in front of the Myrtle Beach Pavilion, tears running down her cheeks, shoulders slumped. That'll get to me every time.

The Pavilion is Myrtle Beach's answer to Coney Island, and a very short answer it is. What with the pavilion and the rides across the street, the place bustles at night with tourists and tons of kids, and you can't walk more than ten feet before bumping into a cop. Myrtle Beach appears to have figured out what its visitors want because the Grand Strand is slammed from Memorial Day until Labor Day, people coming from as far away as Canada.

The night I ran into Nancy, the heat of the day was only an unpleasant memory and the breeze was from the ocean. The Grand Strand was in fine form. Music blared from The Attic, a second-story dance hall where teenagers are protected from adults, and vice versa. At ground level ropers competed for their parents' attention, and up and down the Strip, testosterone-powered cars with thudding basses— backed up for miles—crept past where Nancy Noel sat, tears running down her cheeks.

Wave after wave of pedestrians flooded across the street, some heading for the Pavilion, others leaving the beach for the rides on the other side. Nancy was surrounded by teenagers of all sizes and colors, real clotheshorses or those not wearing much at all. All these kids were laughing or cutting the fool, especially around parents of preteens, who were catching a vision of *their* children's future.

Nancy is a sizable blonde, well past thirty, but without a line on her face. It's as if life passed her by, and in fact, life has. In short, she's long on looks but short on brains. Yes, yes, I know—just the kind of girl any man would find desirable—and that's where I come into the picture. I've been running interference for Nancy for as long as I can remember, and I'm ten years her junior.

Someone had to do something, and do it now, because the poor girl sat where the street dead-ended onto the boardwalk. Though she was crying her eyes out, the cops were blatantly ignoring her—which meant they'd already asked what the problem was and determined it wasn't any of their business.

Chad Rivers agreed. Chad is the guy I've been dating lately and people say we're an item. Anyone I spend more than a couple of weeks with during the Season is serious stuff, and there were those in my circle hinting I should take Chad more seriously. Probably because he was good-looking as well as rich.

Chad and I were about to cross the street and make our way through the amusement park on our way to Mother Fletcher's, a local rock 'n' roll joint, when I spotted Nancy on the curb. I drifted over, pulling Chad with me. His hand came off my butt and slid higher, taking my arm.

"Now what?" he asked.

Chad was irritated because everybody and his sister

seemed to know me and wanted to chat me up. What can I do? I grew up around here—at least since I was fifteen, about the same time my father fell off our fishing boat and drowned. Becoming an orphan at fifteen makes you grow up in a hurry.

So I know my way around and I don't like to be told what to do. Well, maybe I should let Chad. He's got broad shoulders, narrow hips, and a tight little butt. Dark and thoughtful brown eyes—dark and thoughtful for the rich and good-looking, I might add.

"Hon, there's someone I need to see."

When there was a break in the flow of pedestrians across the Boulevard, he saw Nancy on the curb. "No way," he said, gripping my arm. "I didn't bring you here to mother hen anyone."

I let him hold me up, then returned the favor by running my hands from his hips to under his arms. *Numero Uno* wore a black silk shirt and it lay on him as I might later tonight if things worked out. "Chad, it's Nancy."

"It's always someone," he said, gripping me firmly at the waist. "Well, I'm Chad and I'm right here. What are you going to do about it?" he asked with a wicked smile and those beautiful brown eyes of his. He ran long-fingered hands up my sides, touching my breasts.

Catching my breath, I said, "I've got to check on Nancy."

"No, you don't. She's just sitting there, waiting for the next sailor to come along."

"We don't have any sailors in Myrtle Beach, except for you." Chad and his father build boats. Rivers Watercraft is the name of the company and it's located farther inland.

"Whatever. She's waiting for the next 'whatever' to come along. She's the one who dances at the topless joint, isn't she?"

"Chad, why are you being this way?"

"Because I don't know any other way to be. This'll be the fourth person you've stopped and talked to." He glanced at the girl on the curb. Tears still ran down her cheeks and she didn't attempt to wipe them away. "I'm tired of sharing you."

"Mother Fletcher's isn't going anywhere."

He sighed, his hands coming off me. "And neither am I, it would appear."

"This'll only take a moment." I left him and went over to where Nancy sat on the curb, just around the corner from the main drag. If she'd been on the Strip, she would've lost her toes by now. As I said, this time of night the road is slammed with cars.

Nancy wore sandals, red short shorts, and a white halter holding up her substantial chest. Her face brightened when she saw me. "Hi, Susan."

I pulled a Kleenex from my fanny pack. Kneeling, I wiped her childlike face. "Why the tears?"

"Sammy and I had a fight." She gestured toward the amusement park on the other side of the street. Nancy's son was just over four feet tall, with neatly combed hair. He wore a light blue short-sleeved business shirt open at the neck with a pale yellow sweater looped around his neck, its arms tied across the chest. His slacks were charcoal gray and belted, and on his feet were a pair of loafers with no socks.

"What's the problem?"

"He doesn't want to ride the rides."

"And you couldn't ride by yourself?"

"Susan, it's not as much fun when you ride by yourself. You asked me not to have a boyfriend and I don't." Her face brightened. "Will you ride with me?"

"Actually I'm with Chad. Maybe another time."

Her mouth twisted into another pout. "I don't embarrass you, do I, like I embarrass Sammy?"

"No, no." I said, glancing over my shoulder at Chad, who was trying to keep his cool.

"Sammy says I embarrass him."

"All parents embarrass their children or they're not doing their job." I stood up. "I'll go over and have a talk with him."

But when I stepped toward the curb, Chad caught my arm. "Where are you going now?"

"I need to catch Peanut."

"Peanut?" His hand tightened on my arm. "Now who the hell's 'Peanut?'"

"Her son," I said, gesturing at Nancy. "He's the little kid who . . . ." I looked across the street, but the boy was gone. All I saw were the pedestrians jousting with the cars cruising the Boulevard. "He should be riding the rides with his mother."

"And I should be dancing with you. You know, you're not making this easy."

"What? Dancing?"

"No—taking us seriously."

I studied this guy with the mop of hair always out of control. I had the urge to reach up and brush his hair back, and on several occasions had done just that. "I didn't know we *were* serious, Chad."

"And I don't think we'll ever be with you planting these roadblocks in our way."

"Roadblocks?" I asked, as someone jostled me on their way down the sidewalk.

His hand dropped from my arm. "But don't worry, I get the message. Girl as attractive as you, I guess you can have more than one boyfriend with the job you have."

"What are you talking about? I didn't have any idea you were the least bit serious . . . ."

"Why do you think I've been spending all this time scheming to see you—without appearing to be coming on too strong? I see you on your lifeguard stand—your 'throne' as you call it—with all the guys hitting on you. Out of town, inland, they all do. I thought if I didn't come on too strong . . . but that won't work, will it? You're used to the direct approach."

"I didn't know you were this interested—"

"Because you couldn't hear me over the noise of all those guys. It's been nice, Susan. Later."

"Chad?"

And he was gone, disappearing into the crowd.

I was left too stunned to speak. Rock 'n' roll poured out of The Attic, the ropers touted the vices of their bars, and the *thud-thud-thud* of car stereos drowned out all possibility of pleas for Chad to return.

"That your new boyfriend?" asked Nancy, getting to her feet.

"He appears to have been more than a friend. I just didn't know it."

"You didn't?"

And maybe that was *my* problem. I had no clue Chad Rivers was serious about me. We'd only been dating, what was it . . . ? A month ago he'd stopped by my lifeguard stand— no, that'd been . . . before Memorial Day. Now it was approaching August.

I'd thought it was simply another dalliance of a rich boy with a girl from the wrong side of the beach. Chad Rivers was so good-looking and rich he could have any girl on the beach. But evidently he'd chosen me.

"Now you can ride the rides with me."

"Nancy, I think I'd better go after Chad."

"Susan, that's not fair. You don't want me to have a boy-friend, but you have one."

So I rode the rides with her.

The next time I saw Nancy, she was sitting on another sidewalk, propped up against a storefront, ice cream run-ning down her face. Rocky Road, I do believe.

I felt self-conscious at seeing Nancy again—because I was with you-know-who, so I didn't speak as Chad reached for the door of a place where they let you make your own sun-daes. Nancy, however, wasn't as insensitive as I was and flashed a big smile.

"Hi, Susan."

Nancy had her blond hair pulled into a ponytail. She wore a blue tank top and white shorts, the dark ice cream spotting both. Her feet were bare and her legs splayed in front of her.

Stopping at the door that had been opened for me, I asked, "Sammy inside?"

Nancy nodded.

Chad muttered, "Who cares?"

I bit my lip and let Chad's hand at my waist propel me

into the Sundae Shoppe. I wasn't about to have a replay of the scene at the Pavilion. Two weeks earlier I'd swallowed my pride and driven inland to where Chad and his father build their boats. When Chad had come into the reception room, I saw that he wore a long-sleeved, highly starched striped shirt with a loud tie and matching suspenders. His pants were too baggy for his tight little ass, and falling over the brow of his narrow face was the mop of brown hair that always needed to be brushed back.

"Susan?" He looked around. "What are you doing here?" The receptionist eyed us. So this was the gal the boss's son talked about all the time—or so I hoped.

"Chad, you know all those times you said you just happened to be in the neighborhood and dropped by my lifeguard stand to say 'hello'?"

"Er—yes."

"Well, I just happened to be in your neighborhood and thought I'd stop by and say 'hello.' Hello, Chad." And I turned on my heel and walked out the door.

He caught up with me in the parking lot as I was climbing into my jeep.

"Er—Susan, would you like to . . . ?" He looked around. The parking lot was full of cars and pickups—I was in his daddy's space—and behind the cars and trucks stood something resembling an airplane hangar where the watercraft were assembled. A thirty-footer was in there now. It sold for more than three thousand a foot.

"Er—would you like to grab a bite of lunch?"

"If you'd like to," I replied rather coolly. I didn't think Chad could hear the thumping of my heart—unless the sucker burst from my chest. A chest I certainly hoped he noticed—from where I sat in my jeep, chest-at-his-eye-level, wearing cutoffs cut off up to you-know-where. But you have to like your women big. I have the shoulders that come from pulling people ashore who've tried to drown themselves, and I'm taller than most, with gray-blue eyes and sun-bleached hair.

He said, "I know a place if you like barbecue. It's one of

those out-of-the-way places. Really out in the woods."

"Then climb in."

"Er—I thought I might drive."

"Okay with me." I spoke as casually as possible. But climbing down I felt dizzy. The last few days all I could think of was how this guy thought we were an item—and I'd missed it, completely goofed.

Chad led me over to his Corvette and opened the door for me. Before he did he gave me a peck on the cheek. "I've missed you, Susan."

"And I, you," was all I could get out as the tingle reached my toes. But they didn't curl. No. That never happens until he tries to stick his tongue down my throat. Yes, that'll do it every time.

That's just what I was anticipating when we ran into Nancy again. Perhaps I have a death wish because I asked Chad to check the men's room. Sammy was nowhere to be seen. The ice cream parlor was nothing more than a long shaft of a room with a counter running down the middle and tables jammed up against the wall. Over the tables were mounted posters of girls with larger smiles and skinnier than I'd ever be. But I didn't come here for the décor. Or the yogurt.

Chad gave me a sour look before going off toward the rear of the room while I pretended to check out the selection. Nancy shouldn't be left alone, and several times I'd made her promise to stop going out alone. Lost in my thoughts, I didn't hear my boyfriend return.

"He's in there. Now, can we make our sundaes?"

"Sure." I slipped my arm inside his and leaned in close. "And thanks, big fella."

"For nothing."

"Oh, for something." I continued to smile. "Most guys wouldn't understand."

"What makes you think I do?"

But when I spied Nancy starting across the parking lot of the ice cream parlor, I bolted for the door.

"Susan!"

"I'll be right back!" It had not been lost on me that Peanut had not come out of the rest room.

At the sidewalk I caught up with her. Nancy was strolling along, oblivious to everything, and humming the theme from *Flashdance*. Oh, well, where she worked she heard a lot of that.

"Nancy!"

When she turned around, her eyes brightened.

"Oh, hi, Susan."

"Where you going?"

Several guys catcalled and whistled as their sports car raced by on Kings Highway. Nancy waved, then returned her attention to me. "Why, I'm going home."

Instead of telling the little fool she was over five miles from home, I asked, "What about Peanut?"

"Sammy doesn't like that name."

"At school he does and that's where he got it. I thought you said he was in the rest room."

Nancy looked at where a line of cars was parked.

"Then I don't have to walk home." And she headed back in the direction of the ice cream parlor. Jeez, talk about a short attention span.

When we returned to the parking lot, I saw Peanut behind the wheel of a dark blue sports car several yards farther down the strip mall.

"Is he old enough to drive?"

"Until dark," his mother said proudly, then waved in his direction. "Hi, Sammy!"

Peanut didn't return the wave but sat motionless as I reentered the ice cream parlor. On my mind was what I'd have to do to make this up to Chad. Last time it'd been a rather strenuous bit of penance, wilting not only the guy, but his highly starched shirt. We never did find the barbecue joint. Then again, maybe it never existed. By then we had other things on our minds.

2

A few weeks later, I was sitting on my throne and over-looking a dark and desolate kingdom when a tiny voice called up to me.

"Can you help me find my mother?"

It was a blustery day at the beach. The yellow flag up, lots of whitecaps, and the line separating sea from sky blurred by fog rolling ashore. But fools, generally from Canada or somewhere up north, insisted on getting their money's worth. They frolicked where the ocean rushed ashore and kicked up a spray that was immediately caught by the wind and flung inland, many times in my face.

My short blond hair was damp and I hadn't taken off my jacket since arriving. My Egg McMuffin was fully soaked and my coffee cold. The afternoon had turned into a day life-guards hate—lousy weather and no work—the day lasting forever and no guys to hit on you and pass the time. A few good streaks of lightning and I'd pack up the umbrellas, put away the chairs, and be out of here.

The tiny voice repeated itself, asking me to find his mother. I scanned the beach from my perch five feet above the sand.

10

"Where'd you last see her?" I asked.

"At the Open Blouse."

Now that got my attention. The Open Blouse was a top-less joint on the main drag into Myrtle and under constant scrutiny by the local gendarmes and the most vigilant church groups.

I looked down. The kid looking for his mom stood just over four feet tall with windblown, sandy hair and a round, tan face atop a skinny frame. He was dressed in a light blue short-sleeve shirt open at the neck. A woven brown belt held up a pair of slacks on his almost nonexistent hips. He wore cordovan loafers and no socks.

Peanut.

"How long's she been gone this time?"

"A week."

"A week? And you're just telling me now?" I gripped the arms of the stand and eyed the boy, remembering where I'd last seen him. It had been at Wacca Wache Landing where my boat, *Daddy's Girl*, and Harry Poinsett's schooner were moored beside each other. "You've been spending too much time with Dads," I told him.

"Harry Poinsett is like a father to me."

"Have you filed a missing person's report?"

He shook his head.

"Checked the hospitals and the morgue?"

Sammy only stared up at me.

"Well, what *have* you and Harry been up to?" Harry Poinsett is a retired diplomat who lives on a schooner he runs up and down the Intracoastal Waterway. That's a collection of rivers and canals that meanders through Florida, the Carolinas, and up the East Coast.

"We sailed all the way to Florida this time." Sammy's chest proudly expanded.

"Let me guess. You hung around the boat, cleaning up, doing anything not to go home—before Harry made you go check on you mother."

"The lady next door keeps an eye on her."

Color Me Gone

"Only because Dads and I pay her." I glanced at my watch. It was more than an hour before I could put away the umbrellas and chairs.

Crap, Nancy, what've you done this time? They were having that strike at the Open Blouse . . . . Damn! I told you not to join the strikers. Rednecks can become awfully nasty when you threaten their livelihood—or strike their favorite topless joint. And her son had been too embarrassed to return to the Landing and tell Harry his mother was missing. For that he had come to me.

The kid was staring out to sea as the wind ruffled his coiffured hair and whipped at the cuffs of his tailored pants. "Lifeguarding is such a dead-end job," he said.

"Peanut, have you checked where your mother works? Asked the woman next door where she might've gone? Done anything?"

"My mother," he said, watching the surfers capitalizing on their sticks, "she's out-and-out stupid, but you, you don't have to stoop to this."

"Peanut, I asked you a question."

He looked at me. "You know I don't like that name."

"Just answer the question."

"If you took people's advice you'd be farther along in life. I've heard Harry Poinsett—when you don't think I'm listening—tell you that you should leave this line of work."

"Listen, Peanut, I'd love to sit around and sharpen our knives on each other, but nowhere does it say I have to take garbage off some kid who can't handle how his mother makes her living."

"You mean by letting men put their hands all over her?"

I glared at him from my chair.

"Okay, okay," he said, raising his hands. "She doesn't do that. She just dances in their laps."

"Come back in an hour. We'll start then—if you haven't put her out of your mind again."

"I could never forget my mother," he said, starting away. "She won't let me."

12

Steve Brown

Jeez. I was known as a hard case, but this kid had me
beat. "Still attending that private school in Georgetown?"
Georgetown was the snooty town to the south of us, but
never got above its station in life because it lay too close to
Charleston, the mother of all snobs. "And spending your
mother's money faster than it comes in."

The boy stopped and faced me.

"I'll see you at four."

He started walking away again.

"And, Peanut?"

He stopped again but didn't look at me.

"Stop hanging around Harry Poinsett so much. You're even
beginning to sound like him."

Sammy said nothing, only plodded off through the sand
to a ramp that lent easy access to the beach. There he took
off one of his loafers and shook out the sand. When he saw
me watching, he quickly slipped the shoe back on, forcing it
over the heel and hurrying off toward his car, the dark blue
Mustang I'd seen in front of the Sundae Shoppe.

Shit, Nancy, gone over a week? I don't remember your
ever being gone that long. But I remember your being gone a
couple of nights many years ago and your mother calling me
almost nuts with worry. She had good reason. I found you
walking the streets, disoriented and hurting, not understanding what you'd done to make your friend become so violent.

As a teenager Nancy had been studious to a fault: straight
A's on the ol' report card; always at home or in the library;
and working on stuff for extra credit. I met Nancy only after
what was referred to as her "accident."

Nancy was the twin of Jerri: one girl cheery and carefree,
and the other introverted and shy—but not for long. Nancy
became jealous of the popularity of her outgoing twin and
substituted herself on a date with a boy Jerri had dated only
once or twice.

It had been close: showering, fixing her hair, and having
her makeup done; but Nancy knew Jerri was never ready

13

when her date arrived. Many times Jerri would be upstairs bragging to her twin about what she might do that night. That night Nancy learned how much fun sister Jerri was really having.

After a bit of coaxing, Nancy was dropping acid with the best of them, flying higher than most, crashing harder than anyone, and landing in the local hospital. When she was released, there were two carefree girls instead of one, and this only accentuated the fault lines in an already troubled family. Nancy Noel would be forever young, eventually younger than the son conceived that reckless night.

When Nancy had been admitted to the hospital, pregnancy was the last thing on the minds of the staff—with their patient trying to escape through a plate glass window and landing on the roof of the cafeteria one floor down. Three months later, Nancy was tossing her breakfast. Six months after that, Peanut was born. Nancy wasn't capable of raising a kid. Then Jerri left, touring honky-tonks across the Southeast and shaking her tambourine, among other things, on stage. Her mother and father split up over the latter's heavy drinking, and soon Nancy and Sammy were being shuffled back and forth between the two households, if you could call them that. Finally, Mr. Noel dropped out of the picture, sister Jerri was knifed to death in a bar in South Georgia, and her mother was left to care for Nancy—and a grandson. It didn't take long for employers to learn which one of the Noel women would show up for work on a regular basis. The cheerful daughter. So Nancy went to work, and her mother stayed at home and watched her grandson and did some serious drinking.

Nancy worked at one menial job after another with little complaint while Mrs. Noel sank further into alcoholism. Finally, the family was reduced to using food stamps. But cheerful Nancy was always there, working at the Food Lion— where I first ran into her. It wasn't hard to like this girl. She didn't have a mean bone in her body; it was the other parts of her body that were catching guys' eyes.

The owner of a topless bar took note and soon my slow-witted friend was up on stage—if that's what you want to call it—taking off her clothes to the encouragement of a noisy crowd. Nancy thought it all a great hoot, but didn't understand that a person who lives off her looks had best plan for the future. I caught her act once, and the boy with me said my friend was quite good. The whole thing made me want to go home and take a bath.

But I digress. Harry Poinsett and I used some of Nancy's money to enroll Peanut in third grade at Ravenwood Academy. We were anxious to get Sammy out of a house where his grandmother had drowned in her own bath, and his mother might not come home at night. Sammy had been at Ravenwood ever since, coming home only for holidays and summers. During those times, Sammy sunk into a depression over how his mother financed his education. So he became an industrious student at school, running with the smart set at Ravenwood, but turning into a troubled youth at home. Making him even more schizoid was the nickname given to him by his classmates, "Peanut." It was also the name kids called him at home. At Ravenwood he treasured the name, but home, only twenty miles up the coast, the name branded him as a diminutive loser. If I knew Harry Poinsett, the trip down the Waterway was his way of giving Sammy something to write about when his teacher asked how he had spent his summer vacation.

I was stuffing the umbrellas into the flotation box that backs up against the dune when I noticed Peanut had not returned. What else was new? The plywood box lies on its side; the folding chairs get strung together with wire and stood up alongside it. They'd need to be strapped down tonight. A storm was blowing in—the most exciting time to take a speedboat ride.

Where the hell was Peanut? My watch showed it was well past four. But Sammy's competition was arriving, a lean muscular fellow with terrific shoulders and dark tan, taking his daddy's latest boat out for a spin. A cigarette boat, once the darling of the smuggling trade, now the new toy of the Baby Boomers with more money than good sense. Chad almost ran down a surfer as he plowed ashore, waved at me, and leapt off the bow to the shouts of the angry surfers. He gave them all a friendly wave.

Rain blowing in behind him, he shouted, "Time to boogie, Susan."

I slammed the lid on the flotation box. Damn irresponsible for Peanut not to show when he knew I was worried about his mother. Or was I simply pissed about having to ditch this hunk for a dimwitted woman who might not be lost at all, just shacked up with her latest admirer. Thank God, I'd been able to talk Nancy into having her tubes tied. I didn't think I could stand another Peanut.

Damp brown hair hung over Chad's forehead and the collar of his sky blue wetsuit. Chiseled features, dark eyes, and a deep tan, he radiated power and energy, especially after busting his way through all that chop. I had no idea why this guy was interested in me.

"I would've been here sooner, but there was heavy traffic on the river. Everyone's coming inland."

Looking out to sea, I asked, "You really think we should go out?"

"Aw, that's nothing. I've been out in worse."

"I don't know . . . ." I wasn't looking at the ocean now.

"What's the problem?" He grinned. "Scared? Never thought I'd see the day."

"Chad, I don't think I can make it."

"Why's that?" he asked, wiping his forehead and shaking out his hair, my information not registering.

"Something's come up."

Chad gestured at the boat with its narrow slot where we'd be shoved together in familiar intimacy. "I can wait. How long's it going to take?"

"This could take some time."

"Well, hell, Suze, call Marvin and tell him we won't lose

his damn walkie-talkie. If it falls overboard, I'll reimburse him."

"Er—it's not my boss. It's me."

"I don't understand."

"I've . . . I've got to find someone."

He gestured at the water. "But wouldn't you rather ride those waves? We'll show those surfer boys what fun really is."

Jeez. This guy was really excited and the rush was infectious. However, I could still remember the last time I'd found a bruised and battered Nancy. "I—I'm really sorry, Chad, but I can't do this."

"Are you serious?"

"I have to find someone . . . ." I didn't dare mention who that someone was.

"Well, dammit, you could've let me know."

"It came up less than an hour ago and you were already on the river."

He glanced at the lifeguard stand. "You should have a phone out here."

I turned away, snapping the lock on the flotation box. "That would be a violation of Marvin's rules."

"When did you ever care about rules?"

I said nothing. If this guy and I were going to be involved, he'd have to understand my work always comes first. My friends even before that.

Chad looked at hotel row. "You could've gone inside and called. There are plenty of phones in there."

"You know I can't leave the beach."

"If you wanted to you could. You do all the time for lunch."

"This didn't come up at lunch, and someone covers for me . . . then."

But Chad was gone, stomping toward his boat, which the surfers had been staring at, a delicious piece of machinery they'd each like to own.

I wanted to call after him, but I didn't. After all, how far does a gal get by chasing any man?

From where the waves broke over his deck shoes, Chad raised his voice over the surf. "I knew you were hard to get, Susan, but not this difficult. What is it with you—some kind of gauntlet you make your boyfriends run?"

"I have to do this," I said, moving in his direction. At that very moment I realized Chad Rivers wouldn't be coming back. There'd be no reason for me to drop by his father's place of business and tease him with pleasures of my flesh. I had had my first, second, and third chances and blown them all to hell.

"Whoever you want to go looking for can wait a few hours. If they're worth finding at all."

I continued toward the water. "I'll call you, after I find Nan . . . her."

"Why?" he asked, stepping into the slot, into the spot I was supposed to have occupied. "Guys told me, people in my crowd—usually I don't listen to them. But they were right. You use this private eye stuff so you never have to hook up. I thought it'd be different with me."

"You . . . you are different."

He didn't hear me, as he had already cranked the engine, slamming it into gear and backing the cigarette boat into the ocean. And when a cigarette boat is gone, it really leaves you. I could only stand there, with the wind and rain in my face, and watch the boat disappear like a rocket, and wonder if Chad saw my face on each and every wave he smashed through.

3

I arrived at the Open Blouse during the strip joint's happy hour, and wasn't that a thrill: hanging with a bunch of horny guys browsing there instead of Home Depot where they'd told their wives they'd be.

During the summer the traffic is horrendous, yet not much better in spring or fall as people migrate to the Sunbelt. An upscale shopping area called Barefoot Landing led to Dolly Parton's Dixie Stampede, then to the Ronnie Milsap Theater and Broadway at the Beach. Now we are the Branson, Missouri, of the East Coast. Except we have a beach and that compounds our problem. With a squall passing through, it took me over a half hour to drive from the beach to where the damn strip joint was located.

The parking lot was packed with sport utility vehicles, pickups, and late model cars parked cheek to, well, cheek. All this in front of a freestanding, two-story building with a gray stucco front dominated by a door in the shape of a "V," a crude rendering of a woman's open blouse with the collar thrown back.

At the v-shaped entrance, two young women wearing clear

plastic raincoats over bikinis were holding golf umbrellas and helping men negotiate the V. And being fondled for their effort. Anticipation of things to come for the men going inside. For those heading home to their wives, busy with the kids and supper, those busy wives might wonder why their husbands were spending so much time in the bathroom.

The heavier of the two young women wore a red bikini. The other wore a pattern of stars and stripes barely large enough to cover each boob. Both were blond, statuesque, and a bit meaty-looking, if you asked me. A roll of fat oozed over the lower half of the heavier girl's bikini, and the other girl had more moles on her face than Cindy Crawford. In contrast to the girls at the door, a slender redhead stood near the highway under a tarp holding a sign: Organized Workers Are Healthy Workers.

Organizing a topless joint—what chance did these fools have—and in a right-to-work state to boot? The redhead wore the same scanty outfit as the door girls. Hmm. Using sex to sell labor. Wonder what Jimmy Hoffa would think about that?

The girls at the door looked down their noses at me as I approached the V. It made me realize I still wore my nylon rain gear with the white Red Cross emblem across the back, a fanny pack on my hip, soaked running shoes, and a baseball cap pulled down tightly. My bangs were plastered across my forehead.

The heavier of the two, the one in the red bikini, said, "Deliveries are made around back, sister." She spoke with a distinct Yankee accent; another Northie clogging the local highways and byways. Behind her came the sound of blaring music: Mick Jagger wailing he couldn't get no satisfaction.

"Looking for the boss," I said, trying to step inside, careful to avoid their umbrellas.

They closed ranks, blocking my way. "He won't see you," said Red Bikini. "And you can't go inside looking like that. It would ruin the ambience."

"Ambience? What the hell you talking about? This is a strip joint. Besides, this is a public place. You can't keep me out."

The other girl jerked a thumb toward the hallway behind them. "But Harold can."

"Then bring on the asshole. If you girls haven't noticed, it's raining out here." The place didn't have a shelter over the door. No. That would take away from the ambience of the place.

"Hey, Harold," yelled the heavy girl into the hallway. "Got a problem here."

Talk about playing hell with the ambience. Customers were dashing from their cars toward the opening in the . . . blouse, while us gals blocked the way, a catfight brewing.

A heavyset young man appeared at the door. His black hair was pulled into a ponytail and he wore, of all things, a tux. "What you need?" *His* voice was Southern-fried, but he was still probably clogging up the highways, if not his own arteries. The big fellow sported a stomach that strained his cummerbund.

"Need to see the boss," I said, moving away from the door so that customers could pass.

The bouncer looked me over, then sidestepped three guys being escorted through the V by the scantily clad girls. One of the threesome copped a feel of the heavier girl's ass. She didn't seem to mind. Matter of fact, her smile grew larger, as did, I suppose, some part of the guy.

"Who you looking for? Your husband?" Harold had to raise his voice over the music coming down the hallway. "What's his name? I'll have him sent out."

"Nah. I'm here to see the boss."

"But you don't have an appointment."

"How you know I don't?"

"Mr. Flaxx don't see nobody this late in the day," explained the heavier of the two girls, returning to her post.

"Salesmen have to see him before or after lunch," the bouncer went on.

"So off you go, sister," said Red Bikini.

I turned on her. "You have something to offer to the conversation or just looking for a friendly poke on the jaw?"

The girl blinked and stepped back. Top heavy on her spike heels, she stumbled against the partition making up one side of the blouse. The girl in the stars and stripes bikini had to steady her.

Harold thrust his huge stomach between us. "Okay, okay. We don't want any trouble here. We've got customers to think about."

I continued to glare at the woman in the red bikini. "Oh, there wasn't going to be any trouble. More like a little attitude adjustment. Look, Harold, all I want to know is the last time Nancy Noel showed up for work."

"Nancy Noel?"

"Yes," I said, suddenly tiring of this whole affair. Or maybe realizing I'd really mucked things up with Chad and he might never come back. That thought wasn't far from my mind—ever. "You can tell me that, can't you?"

The girl in the red bikini glanced at the bouncer. A worried look crossed her face.

"A couple of weeks ago," said the fat man. "Mr. Flaxx had to fire her."

"She was talking up that strike," volunteered the heavy girl, sticking her face through the V. "I heard her. Don't tell me I didn't. I know what I heard."

"Are you sure you've got the right girl?" I asked.

"Yeah," Harold said, "and you don't want to talk to Mr. Flaxx about those people."

"Why's that?"

He pointed at the tarp where the demonstrator stood with her sign against her legs. The rain was really coming down now, pockmarking puddles near the striker's shelter.

"Nancy was one of Mr. Flaxx's favorites. It really pissed him off—her striking."

"And she's not getting her job back," said Red Bikini, and very quickly, too.

"Oh. Now I get the picture."

"What's there to get?" asked the girl in red. "Your friend couldn't keep her mouth shut and got tossed out on her can."

"Uh-huh."

"And what's that supposed to mean?" asked the girl in the stars and stripes. "It's the truth, even if you don't believe it. Harold, I think she's a troublemaker, like her friend."

"I guess you better move along, lady. You don't want to be upsetting Mr. Flaxx."

"No, no. We wouldn't want that." There'd always be time to speak to the owner of this frigging whorehouse. Besides, the woman walking the picket line could probably tell me more about Nancy than any of these assholes. "Tell your boss I'll be back."

The fat man came down the steps behind me. "Just who are you, lady? Vice? Health inspector? The boss—he don't like no surprises."

"Then he's in for a real treat when he meets me."

I left Harold where the concrete ended and crossed the parking lot, skirting the larger puddles. A gust from the squall lifted up the bill of my baseball cap and hit me square in the face. Pulling my hands out of my pockets, I wiped my face and finished crossing the parking lot.

The shelter had a green plastic top, four poles, pegs, and lines holding it up. One of the pegs had loosened and the side it was responsible for had collapsed. I doubt anyone had told this girl that walking a picket line at the beach in the middle of the summer would make her feel so utterly miserable.

Though her shoulders were hunched, the redhead was as tall as me—nearly five-foot-ten. She had blue eyes and a skinny, freckled frame. The fact that her chest offered little to brag about made me wonder if she'd joined the strike because she couldn't cut it in the building behind me. Some would say that was a cruel thing to say about any woman, but hell, life is cruel to each and every woman in its own special way.

The redhead occupied a muddy piece of ground so near the curb that water puddled up from cars speeding by. "What do you want?"

"Do you mind if I step inside—out of the rain?"

"Are you from the paper? The media has ignored us."

"Not with the paper. I just want to ask some questions."

"We have a right to be here."

"Look, I don't care—"

"You have no right hassling us." She held out her sign. The poster was slapped into her measly chest by the gusting wind. The tarp rustled. "We have a right to the first ten feet from the street. The court said so."

"I'm not with the Open Blouse."

"Then who are you?"

"Susan Chase," I said, stepping under the tarp and out of the rain. "I'm a lifeguard at Myrtle Beach."

"If you're inquiring about a job, I can tell you that you can make a lot of money, but you won't have any benefits. Or get any respect."

Especially from me. "I'm a friend of Nancy Noel."

"Nancy? Nancy was supposed to pull this shift. We do four hours on, eight off, so there's always someone here. She hasn't shown up for several days."

"You're here alone?" Morals are always lower where men patronize sex joints and I personally wouldn't want to risk being here alone, especially after dark.

Across the highway I noticed a strip mall that sold baskets, pottery, linens, and discount shoes. One of the cars at the edge of its parking lot was a dark blue Mustang, and in the front seat sat Sammy Noel.

"No, no," said the redhead, "there're always two of us after dark or we have instructions to take down the tarp and leave. And bring along the sign. Well, that's the way it's supposed to work, but with Kathy gone and some of the others dropping out, I don't know exactly what the rules are. We need more volunteers. Listen, if you're serious about working topless, you owe it to yourself to make sure they offer you benefits."

Instead of telling her I had no intention of taking off my clothes in front of a bunch of horny guys, I asked, "What are your demands?"

The redhead drew herself up to her full five-foot-ten and almost hit her head on the billowing tarp. "Everyone has rights and one of them is to unionize."

"Yeah, but at a strip joint?"

"It's not a strip joint. It's a topless bar. Look, Miss . . . ?"

"It's Chase. Susan Chase. And your name?"

"Lollie Lloyd. It's a stage name." She glanced at the building behind her. "Daryl—I mean, Mr. Flaxx gave it to me. He said it sounded better than Rebecca or Becky Lloyd. Look, Miss Chase, what do you really want?"

"I just want to find Nancy. Her son says she's missing." I glanced across the highway. The Mustang was gone, along with my own private stalker.

"Try her house. But I don't think she's there. I've called several times and all I get is the machine."

"Then where?" I'd called the house while driving over and had also gotten Nancy's machine.

"Who knows? Maybe she dropped out, like Kathy."

"Kathy? Who's that?"

"Kathy Gierek—the one who organized the strike."

"When did she leave?"

"A couple of weeks ago."

"And it didn't seem suspicious that two of your friends disappeared within a week of each other?"

The redhead shrugged and the sign slipped out of her hands and fell to the ground. Immediately we both grabbed it. When I let go of my end, she shook it out, splattering me with mud. This simply wasn't my day.

"Oh, I'm sorry." Her hand came up to her throat. "I didn't mean to do that."

"No problem." I wiped flecks of mud off my face. My rain gear was also spotted, along with my legs. "Kathy Gierek?" I asked again.

"Until she dropped out, Kathy was really involved."

"She was your leader?"

"Well, she and me."

"And Nancy?"

"I don't think Nancy approved of the strike."

"Until Flaxx fired her."

"Yeah," she said, glancing at the girls working the door of the Open Blouse. "But that was political."

"So I figured. When was Nancy fired?"

"Oh, a week ago. The first day she was supposed to walk the picket line, she reported for work inside the Blouse. Harold had to explain the she couldn't come in because she'd been fired."

"Where do I find this Kathy Gierek?"

"She has a trailer at Emerald Cove, a mobile home park on the way to Conway."

On the way to Conway. That's where I should have been, chasing down Chad Rivers at his boatyard. "Back to the original question: You didn't think it odd that two of the striking girls disappeared at the—"

"We're women and we have rights!"

"Yeah, right." My feminist hackles had not been raised. Stripping in public—somewhere you have to draw a line.

Lloyd gestured around the sheltered area as the traffic whizzed by, some of it splashing water over the curb where it narrowly missed our feet. "Listen, Miss Chase, this is my livelihood we're talking about. I don't have long to practice my art so it's not right for me not to get what I deserve. Others do. Why not me?"

"Yes—why not?"

"Now you're mocking me. Why don't you try standing outside all day—in the rain?"

Maybe because I'm not that dumb?

"I've been here every single day for at least one shift, ever since the strike began. Not even Kathy's done that, and certainly not Nancy. She couldn't even remember the days she was supposed to walk the picket line."

"When did the strike begin?"

"This is our thirty-third day," she said proudly, "and we're going to break Flaxx. You just watch."

I glanced at the building where four men stumbled out—with their sexy escorts. From inside came the sound of Fat Boy Slim performing "Rockafeller Skank."

"It doesn't look like he's got much to worry about."

"He should be. We're going to put him out of business."

A horn tooted from a passing pickup.

"See," Lloyd said, "people don't like seeing us being pushed around."

"Or they like the view."

"They support us!"

"Then why don't you put on some clothes so you can be sure?" And I sloshed away, crossing the parking lot through several puddles, and all the time watched by the girls in the V of the Open Blouse. One of them chewed on a nail as I climbed into my jeep. The other gave me the finger, down low, beside her, then turned and greeted the next customer with a big smile.

Gee, nothing like getting caught in the middle of a family fight, and wasn't it going to be a kick in the ass when I found Nancy holed up with some guy. And if she'd been raped, well, she'd been raped before, and there was nothing I could do about it but hold her. When that'd happened to me, I'd wanted someone to hold me but not some damn man.

4

Nancy Noel lived in the old cinder block house she'd been raised in. Since then the neighborhood had gone steadily downhill—as far downhill as a cinder block neighborhood can slide. No wonder Peanut spent so much time aboard Harry Poinsett's schooner. The grass needed to be cut and trash was plastered against the side of the house. The place looked deserted. And it was still raining. Nice touch, Mother Nature, you really put me in the mood.

In the yard next door was parked a Toyota pickup with its own set of problems: paint peeling, hood up, and weeds growing around its flat tires. The house on the other side of Nancy's had a new fishing boat parked in the driveway. The woman in that house lived on disability from the paper mill in Georgetown. Despite the weather—or perhaps because of it—she sat in a recliner on a wooden porch and held a beer carelessly. The woman had frizzled yellow hair and wore a lumberjack shirt, and she looked like she'd rather be anywhere than sitting on her front porch. The rain probably had something to do with that. I pulled my jeep alongside Nancy's mailbox and checked for mail.

Empty.

I slammed the mailbox shut and drove into her driveway. Killing the engine, I glanced at the woman in the recliner. She neither moved nor looked in my direction. The old bitch must really be soused. Hard to believe Harry and I paid good money for her to keep an eye on the Noels. After pulling the hood of my rain jacket over my head, I climbed down from my jeep, checked that my fanny pack was secure, and approached the house. By now my feet were thoroughly soaked.

The porch was occupied by the same metal furniture Nancy's mother had bought years ago, now rusted, worn, and cracked with age. Nancy had wanted to buy some new stuff, but Dads and I discouraged her, saying a woman living alone shouldn't advertise her wealth. Take the French Quarter approach, encouraged Harry. Keep it drab and worn on the outside but dress it up inside. Nancy had gone along with the idea because it sounded like such a marvelous game.

A wooden footlocker painted olive drab sat near the front door and held a bag of cat food. Both cat bowls were empty, so I poured some food into one, then placed the other in the rain where it could collect water. A daddy-longlegs ran up my arm as I returned the sack to the footlocker. Brushing off the funny-looking creature, I watched it fall to the concrete and scurry off in search of more friendly environs. When I rang the bell, I got no answer, so I opened the screened door and rapped on the frame.

"Nancy!"

I did some more beating and hollering, and when that brought no response, went to a front window and did the same again.

Couldn't see a damn thing. Curtains covered all the windows, dark ones for sleeping during the day and keeping out the heat—and me. It was then that the woman next-door raised her voice over the rain.

"She left town."

"Left town?" I looked in her direction.

"Yep. She's gone." The woman raised the beer to her lips

and took a long swallow. A cooler sat beside the recliner, and more than one empty lay beside the chair where she'd dropped them. "Her and her boyfriend done gone away."

I stepped down from the porch and crossed the woman's driveway, skirting the new fishing boat. "Have you any idea who her new boyfriend is?"

The woman shook her frizzled head. "Some camel jockey. They left together and he come back and picked up a few things. Had her key and all." She tilted her head and regarded me. "I remember you. What was your name? Sadie? Sally?"

"Chase. Susan Chase."

"Yeah, the smart aleck kid. I kept an eye on your friend like Mr. Poinsett asked. Now he's a real gentleman, Mr. Poinsett. Always addresses me as 'Mrs. Owens.'" She finished her beer and dropped the empty beside the others on the concrete. "And don't even think about asking me to check on the boy. That runt's a little too snooty for my taste."

"Then you won't be needing that check Mr. Poinsett and I've been sending you each month."

"Never did need it." The old woman opened the cooler and reached inside. "And we sure as hell don't need it now." She lost her grip on the beer and had to reach into the cooler to retrieve it. Once done, she sat upright in the chair, fumbled with the tab, and finally opened it. She gave a long, manly burp. "Me and my old man—we got plenty."

"How's that?" I asked, trying to control my anger. I could feel my hands clenching into small balls at my sides and rain running down my cheeks, some of it ultimately finding its way inside my jacket. "You win the lottery?"

She grinned. "That we did."

"You're shitting me."

The woman sat up and the recliner groaned. "Don't be using that kind of language. You're on my property now."

"Sorry, Mrs. Owens, but you don't look that lucky."

She settled back in the chair. "Shows what you know. My old man scratched this little card and won ten thousand dollars, so we won't be needing your money no more. If we ever did."

"And you bought the boat with your winnings?"

"Sure did," she said with another smile.

"Pretty expensive looking piece of equipment," I said, glancing at the boat.

"Nine thousand dollars," she said proudly, "if it were a penny."

"And you kept the rest to pay the taxes?"

"Taxes?" Owens was about to take another pull from her beer. She stopped. "What taxes?"

"Didn't you notice the lottery people asked for your husband's name and address?"

"Yeah." She shifted around in the recliner and it groaned again. "But that was to send us the check. And we cashed that sucker, too." Again she grinned.

"And your husband had to give the state his social security number."

She frowned. "I don't know nothing about that."

"Well, ask your husband. I'll bet he ran all the way to the post office and mailed in his social security number that very same day."

To this she said nothing, but I could sense the wheels turning in her inebriated brain.

"Those IRS boys, Mrs. Owens, they want their money. They don't care how you made it—gambling, lotteries, stealing, they just want their share—and one way or the other, they always get it." I glanced at the boat again. "You know, I'm just a smart-alecky kid, but anyone can tell it's going to take catching a mess of fish to pay taxes on a boat that nice."

I left her staring at the boat and waiting for her old man to return. The two of them had some serious catching up to do.

Inside Nancy's house—Nancy always left a key under the mat—the living room was littered with fast food wrappers, soft drink cups, and paper sacks. Nancy didn't cook, and I didn't encourage it since the house was heated by gas and Nancy smoked. Splatters of red and yellow decorated the floor where ketchup and mustard had stained it. A line of ants was carrying off the caked remains of a spilled chocolate milkshake.

But the furniture was new. Nancy bought whatever took her fancy. Sometimes she'd forget what she had, so duplicates filled each room. Big screen TVs were in every room, including the kitchen, and there were so many La-Z-Boys they lined the hallway. Because Nancy slept during the day, the curtains were closed and cobwebs formed in the corners where insects had been snared. When the trash began drawing ants, and the creatures started nipping Nancy's ass, she'd go on a tear and clean up the place. But the corners of the house always remained nasty—cobwebs strung from curtain to corner.

Harry Poinsett said Nancy should have maid service, but I thought she should be responsible for something. And why couldn't she cut the grass or hire a neighborhood boy to do it? Hell, even Peanut might pitch in. There was a lawn mower—maybe more than one—in a metal shed behind the house.

Peanut's bed didn't look like it had been slept in lately, but there was an odor I recognized.

Something dead in here! My heart leaped to my throat as I raced from one room to the other.

"Nancy! Nancy!"

If my friend really was dead, it made absolutely no sense to be shouting her name, but I was pretty wound up. All afternoon I'd been snapping at everyone. Maybe I was pissed at not being with Chad; more likely, frustrated I hadn't agreed with Dads to have Nancy put in some home. But after my experience in a foster home I couldn't see . . . .

Precious.

Nancy's cat. Lying near the back door and on her side. I stared at the poor thing, then swallowed hard and went looking for a dustpan. Precious would have to be buried, and I wondered if Nancy owned a shovel. Shit. She probably owned a dozen.

I was taking the dustpan out of the closet when I heard a voice shouting from outside. Going to the door I saw two cops kneeling behind their patrol cars, shotguns drawn, and calling for me to come out with my hands up.

The bitch next door! It had to be!

"I used a key to get in this place!" I shouted through the open door. Myrtle Beach cops aren't known for blowing away people—they might turn out to be tourists—but you never know.

"That doesn't change a thing," said one of the two cops. "We want you, and anyone else in that house, face down on the porch, facing away from us, hands by your sides, palms up, and ankles crossed."

I cursed, then shouted, "I'm coming out so watch where you're pointing those shotguns."

"We know what we're doing, lady, and you'd better know what you have to do."

I walked onto the porch with my hands over my head, hood down, and running suit blouse tucked in tightly so they could see I was a girl. Their cars were pointed at an angle and they had their slickers on. The rain is why I never heard them arrive. The cops behind the patrol cars held shotguns. The cops I didn't see, those at each side of the door, grabbed me and swung me around, throwing me up against the house.

"Assholes," I muttered, after catching my breath and grabbing a piece of the house.

"Shut up," said a raspy voice over my shoulder. The cop's breath was hot on my ear as he ran his hands up and down my rain gear.

Out of the corner of my eye I saw a fourth cop, a brunette, holding her Glock in a two-handed grip and pointing at my head. Finished with my pat-down, the raspy-voiced cop stripped me of my fanny pack, stepped back, and started searching it. He was a fat guy with a stomach that pushed out his yellow slicker. There was mud on his shoes. All and all, his partner was much more attractive.

"Can I turn around?" I asked.

"Do it," said the fat cop who held my fanny pack. He had holstered his pistol. "Just nothing funny."

I lowered my hands as I turned around. When I did, the Glock was stuck in my face.

"Nothing was said about taking your hands down, honey," said the female with the nine-millimeter.

As my hands went back up I looked around. In the street people had umbrellas up and raincoats on, braving the weather for a better look. The woman next door leaned back in her recliner, beer in one hand and a smile plastered across her face.

Gesturing with my head in the woman's direction, I asked, "Isn't it against the law for people to be drinking out-of-doors?"

"I think it'd be best if you kept your mouth shut, honey," said the female, her weapon still pointed at me.

"There's a gun in here," muttered her partner, fighting with my fanny pack. "I just can't get to it."

"Want me to show you how it's done?"

The brunette tapped me on the shoulder with the barrel of her pistol. "Just stay where you are, honey. Breaking and entering is a serious crime."

"Not when you use a key. It's in my pocket."

Her fat partner tossed my fanny pack on the footlocker and pointed at me. "You—keep your mouth shut."

"Then how'll I answer your questions?"

He pulled back his slicker at the waist and glanced at his shoes. "My feet are soaked so don't give me any crap."

Another cop approached the house through the downpour. Behind him a fourth one reached into his patrol car and returned the shotgun to its ceiling mount.

"That's Susan Chase you've got there," said the cop approaching the house. He was a stocky fellow with muscular arms that stuck out from under his slicker.

"What we've got here is a damn attitude," said the fat cop, "caught in the act of breaking and entering."

"That may be," said the muscular cop, stepping on the porch and stomping water off, "but she helps us locate runaways."

"She does?" asked the female cop with the pistol pointed at my head. "She's just a kid herself."

I snorted. "You're one to talk." The woman with the Glock had a baby face and adorable blue eyes.

"Check her fanny pack," said the cop who had just joined us. "She should have some ID."

"I didn't see any license, Webster, but there's a gun in there."

"Can I lower my hands?"

The baby-faced woman nodded. "But stand where you are, Miss Chase. We have procedures to follow."

The female lowered her pistol, holstered it, then went inside. The fourth cop, who had remained in the car, put down his microphone. He climbed out and began to disperse the crowd. One of the voyeurs was Sammy Noel, and it took more than a few words to move him along. I wanted to call out to Peanut, but I was too disgusted with myself. I'd brought this on myself by jerking around the old lady in the recliner. And she'd jerked back. When would I ever learn?

"What were you doing in the house, Miss Chase?" asked Webster.

"Looking for a friend."

"And you had to break in to do it?" asked the fat cop. His feet must've really been bothering him. He looked awfully pissed.

"Who says I did?"

"We got a call."

"From the woman over there." I gestured at the recliner and the woman with the beer. "I asked her to keep an eye on this place and I paid for the service."

"Then why's she mad at you?" asked Webster, glancing at

the old woman who sat in the recliner.

"Wouldn't you be?" asked the fat cop. "The kid's got an attitude."

"Hey," called the female from inside. "Got an odor. Might have a body in here."

The fat cop stepped over, grabbed me by the shoulders, and twisted me around, flinging me against the house. He kicked my feet apart as I grabbed the front of the house again. "I thought there was something fishy about you."

"Not fish," I said, after catching my breath. "My friend's cat's in there. In the kitchen. Trapped inside without any food or water. And if your partner isn't blind, she'll see where I dropped the dustpan when I was interrupted by you guys."

Webster stepped to the door and shouted, "You got a dead cat in the kitchen?"

"Right," came the woman's voice.

I started to turn around. "Now can I—"

A forearm was stuck across my back, pushing me back into the wall and taking my breath away. "Stay right where you are until my partner finishes checking the house. We're not playing games here."

So I leaned against the face of the house and waited. Minutes later the woman was through with her search and rejoined us on the porch.

"I opened the back door and threw out the cat. There was a dustpan on the hallway floor to pick it up with."

"You threw Precious out?" I turned around and came off the wall. "In the rain?"

"Not in my job description to bury dead animals, honey."

"Yeah. Right. Only rousting law-abiding citizens."

"Look, Webster," asked the fat cop, "you want this call or not? Tucker and I've got others to catch."

Webster looked at me. "Yeah, I'll take it."

"Good, and you, young lady"—the fat cop shook a finger in my face—"watch that attitude or one day somebody's not going to just roust you."

As he turned to leave I stepped over to the footlocker and

picked up my fanny pack. "Hey, don't you want to see my license?"

He faced me. Behind him rain poured off the edge of the porch, splattering in a line chiseled in the ground. "You've taken up enough of my time, kid."

"I insist." I ripped down the velcro side of my fanny pack and the Lady Smith & Wesson fell into my hand. It has a shroud so the hammer won't hook on all the stuff us gals tote around.

The cops reached for their handguns as I twirled the pistol on my trigger finger. "Hey, you were right. There was a pistol in there. A license, too, if you'd cared to look."

"Watch it, Chase," said Webster. His Glock was pointed at me, as were all the others.

"No—you guys watch it. I don't like being pushed around, especially when I'm on the job."

"What job?" asked Webster.

"Looking for a missing person."

"Runaway?"

"No. Missing person." I inclined my head in the direction of the bitch in the recliner. With the appearance of my pistol, her smile had pretty much disappeared. "Like I said, she was supposed to have watched out for my friend. And I paid for the service."

"Then you have a beef with her, not us. Now put that gun away."

I stuck the Smith & Wesson into the fanny pack, velcroed up the side, and fastened it around my waist.

The fat cop watched me put away my weapon. "You know, young lady, I could haul your ass downtown for pulling such a stunt."

"But you won't," I said with a smile. "You've got other calls to catch."

"Damn," said the fat cop, shaking his head. "You'll love this, Webster. You're the bleeding heart type."

After they left, the muscular cop gestured me inside. He looked around while his partner remained in their patrol car and, I suppose, told police dispatch it had all been a false alarm.

"Your friend—what's her name?"

"Nancy Noel."

"You say she's missing?"

"Yes." I looked around the room with its cobwebbed curtain, new furniture, and junk food spoor. "Hasn't been seen for over a week."

"By who?"

"Her son."

"And how old is he?"

"Fifteen."

"And the father?"

"Hasn't had anything to do with the boy for years."

"Not the way I treat my kid, and me and my old lady have been divorced for over five years."

He went down the hallway, glancing in the bedrooms. I followed him, heading for the kitchen. At the back door I stared at Precious lying in a pool of water. Damn. Precious hadn't received any more respect than I had.

Webster came into the kitchen and joined me at the door. "Not a drop of water in the tub. That cat must've really suffered. You know, Miss Chase, there's lots of expensive electronic equipment in this house. New furniture, too. Your friend wasn't in a hurt for money."

"She wasn't into drugs, if that's what you're thinking."

"Where'd you say she worked?"

"I didn't, but it's the Open Blouse. Out on five-oh-one."

"I know where it is." He frowned. "I also know *what* it is. The other guys were right. I am a soft touch."

"Probably because you still have the ability to care."

He went back down the hallway. "Caring about the wrong people can become an occupational hazard in my business, if not a waste of time."

I followed him past the line of La-Z-Boys. "But you'll still file a missing person's report, won't you?"

"Oh, sure," he said, heading for the door. "But truth be

known, I'd say she ran off with her latest john. She couldn't care less about her boy. He's the one I feel for."

I followed him to the porch where he stopped to pull up the hood of his slicker. I said, "You've got part of that right. She was people. Maybe not what a cop thinks is the right kind of people, but she's still a person."

Webster's partner had reached the porch. "What's the story? If it's a false alarm why are you still inside?"

"Because I'm a soft touch."

The other cop looked at me.

"Tell you in the car." Webster headed down the sidewalk through the pouring rain.

The other cop gave me a quizzical look, then followed his partner to the patrol car. As Webster cranked the engine, his partner slid in beside him. And me? I was left with a dead cat to bury and the bitch next door smiling at me from the depths of her recliner.

5

Emerald Cove was two parallel lines of trailers posing as a middle-class subdivision. An entry gate and sign put you on notice that the trailer park was part of a neighborhood crime watch. The Cove had a paved road, neat homes—each with a skirt around its base—flowers, bushes, an occasional tree, and shelters for the cars. I banged on several doors until someone finally opened her door to a hooded figure in Red Cross rain gear whose feet squished when she walked.

"Kathy Gierek?" The person who had taken pity on me was a big, bony woman. An emaciated man peered over her shoulder. "Why, Kathy left here weeks ago. Cleaned out her trailer and was gone. Left a terrible mess and lots of junk. The realtor had a big yard sale, but none of us property owners would buy anything."

"The unit's a rental?"

"It's not supposed to be. The covenant clearly states no rentals. This is a retirement community."

From behind her, the old man nodded.

"But we've gotten up a petition," the old woman went on. "We're going to let those people know we don't want tran-

Steve Brown

sients in our neighborhood. Why, the Carters"—she pointed
down the paved road that ran through the park—"they leased
last year and about never got the woman and her kids out of
the place. Tore the trailer up good, they did." She finished
with a nod that was followed by another from her husband.

"Let all those people stay at the beach, that's what I say.
They're used to handling those kinds of problems. Us—we
don't have the money to be golfing every day. We have to
watch our pennies . . . and our property values." She shot
an angry look over her shoulder at her husband. When she
returned her attention to me, she said, "The Gierek girl
worked in a strip joint. You're not one of those girls, are
you? I don't want my Fred getting any funny ideas."

I could see Fred smile just before his wife stepped back
and shut the door in my face. Soaking wet from running
from jeep to house and back again, not to mention being
rousted by the frigging cops, I heated up at this latest disre-
spect and raised my hand. Before I could hammer on the
door, the curtain in the window nearest me moved. It was
Fred, smiling and pointing to a trailer across the street—
until his wife screeched at him. The curtain fell into place
and Fred's face was gone. I couldn't help but laugh, rain
and all. Then I dashed to my jeep, backed out of their driveway, and into the driveway of the unit formerly rented by
Kathy Gierek.

There was no awning at this unit, so I stood on a wet
deck filled with wet toys and spoke with a barefoot woman,
her hair in rollers and a small child beside her. There was
no security chain between her face and mine—my God, how
can women be so naïve! She held a baby in her arms. The
TV was blaring on about the astonishing good fortune view-
ers had to purchase a "handy dandy"—I didn't catch the
last of the commercial, because the mother screamed over
her shoulder for someone named "Race" to turn down the
TV. That done, we could finally talk.

"Kathy Gierek? She don't live here. I don't know where
she went. Some say she left town. I don't know. Maybe you

41

could check next-door. They might know."

"She didn't leave a forwarding address?"

"I don't know nothin' about that. You'll have to ask the agent. I got this place outta the want ads."

"And the name of the realtor?"

"Devon Real Estate. They've got a place out on the four lane." She gestured with her head toward a room littered with toys. With an embarrassed smile, she added, "I don't think I woulda gotten in here if I'd showed up with all my kids."

A bloodcurdling scream from the interior made me reach for my fanny pack.

The woman yelled at someone I couldn't see. "Race, I told you not to be tying her up like that."

I slid the Smith & Wesson back into my fanny pack, and as I did, vowed never to have kids—at least not like the ones on display here. "Did Kathy leave anything behind?"

The woman shook her head. The baby in her arms gurgled and smiled. He was a cute little thing with a full head of hair and a happy smile. How long would that last with brother Race around?

"Nothing was left behind. They cleaned up the place real good." The woman looked into the room at a place I couldn't see. "I might have to have somebody come in and clean up after us," she added with a nervous laugh. "The kids—they're awful messy with Kool-Aid and chewing gum."

"Does Kathy still get mail here?"

"Yeah, but I don't see it anymore because the mailman turns around and sends it back. I had to tell him several times."

"Back where?"

"If it weren't a bill, all her mail came from Chicago."

"Kathy was from Chicago?"

"She had kin back there. A place called Skokie. Funny name for a town, ain't it?" Another scream and the woman flashed a nervous smile, "Now if you don't mind, Miss, I've got to tend to my young'uns."

"You don't happen to remember the return address, do you?"

There was the sound of breaking glass, followed by some crying; then something hit the wall hard enough to make the trailer rock.

"Lady," said the young mother, "some days I don't even remember my own name."

No one was home next-door. I had better luck with an old woman in the trailer on the far side of the one where the kids were conducting their demolition derby. She was willing to talk and didn't have any husband standing behind her. This trailer had a wooden deck with redwood chairs and a gas grill. The railing's cap was wide enough to hold a row of clay flowerpots filled with geraniums, their saucers overflowing with rain. Every once in a while the wind gusted up and flung water in my face.

"Kathy Gierek? Yes, I knew Kathy." The elderly woman was small of frame but stood erect. She looked to be in her seventies. Her bright sundress exposed wrinkled, suntanned arms, and she wore a touch of makeup on her square-shaped face. "Come in, dear. You shouldn't be out in all this."

Saying "thank you" and throwing back the hood of my jacket, I stepped inside, wiped my feet on a mat inside the door, and noticed a green parrot on a corner perch. Wood paneling covered the walls and balusters separated a small dinette from the kitchen. The tiny kitchen had the usual clean and shiny appliances, which contrasted with the old-fashioned furniture. The walls displayed a photographic gallery of men and women in styles of dress from the turn of the century up to contemporary school photographs. In one corner a wrought iron stand held an urn.

"My former husband," said the old woman, gesturing at the urn. "Mr. Tudor. Though I think he would have preferred burial on the eighteenth hole. Would you like a cup of coffee? It might warm you up. And take off that jacket and hang it behind the door."

"Thank you, Mrs. Tudor, and it's Chase. Susan Chase." I saw pots and pans on the stove. The smells told me the woman was about to eat. She had to be expecting someone. "Maybe I should come back later."

"You'll do no such thing. We old folks don't get much company. I'll fix you a bite."

"No, no, I couldn't—"

From behind me, a coarse, sharp voice said, "Have a seat and set a spell."

I whipped around, my hand slapping the fanny pack. Instantly the gun was in my hand, and just as quickly, my face heated up as the speaker turned out to be the parrot. I quickly velcroed the gun back into the fanny pack. I was a nervous wreck from shotguns and pistols being stuck in my face, running around in this storm, and finding no one who could tell me anything about Nancy.

"Oh, my," said the old woman. "I didn't expect Maggie to frighten you so." She eyed the fanny pack. "Was that a gun I saw, Susan?"

"Mrs. Tudor, I'm trying to locate Kathy Gierek. She might know where I can find Nancy Noel."

"Yes, yes," said Tudor, still staring at my fanny pack. "I heard Kathy speak of her. Nancy was a little slow, wasn't she? Oh, I don't mean that in a mean-spirited way. Er— Susan, would you mind showing me your gun?"

"Pardon?"

"Your pistol. Do you mind showing it to me?"

"It's just a pistol, Mrs. Tudor. A Lady Smith & Wesson."

Again the parrot said to have a seat and set a spell. I thought I might pee in my pants. "I'm keeping you from your dinner." God, but did the stuff on that stove smell good. I hadn't smelled anything like that since I'd located a runaway working in the kitchen of the Radisson.

"Make yourself at home, Susan. I've never met anyone who carries a gun."

"Really, Mrs. Tudor—"

"You show me yours and I'll show you mine." Returning

to the kitchen area, she turned and smiled. "I'll tell you what I know of Kathy Gierek."

The rain hit the trailer with the force of a storm. Did I really want to go out in that and find a McDonald's? From the table I picked up one of the napkins and fingered it.

"Yes—cloth, Susan. I never was comfortable with paper. It doesn't feel right."

"But don't they have to be washed?"

She was dishing food onto plates. The plates were real china and the cabinets real wood; none of that pressed wood shit for Mrs. Tudor. "And what else would I do with my time? I'm always hoping one of my friends will stop by, and now I've got you, I'm not going to let you go. All those photographs in the living room—that's all the company I have. Mr. Tudor wanted to retire to the beach and play golf. He died on the sixteenth hole after making his first hole-in-one. Forty years of golf and never made a hole-in-one." She glanced at the urn across the room. "I hope they have a golf course where he is now." She brought the plate over, then poured coffee in a cup patterned with small roses. "And the children, well, I hate to disappoint them by not living on the beach."

Sighing and shaking my head, I pulled my pistol from my fanny pack, emptied the rounds from the chambers, and placed the weapon on the table next to my silverware.

"Oh, my." Tudor clunked her plate on the table and missed the mat, then scooted it onto the cloth. "Have you ever shot anyone, my dear?"

I shook my head. "Saves wear and tear on the knuckles." I sat down and dug into the string beans, mixing them with the mashed potatoes in my haste to inhale real food for a change.

"You would actually hit someone?"

"Now that," I said with my mouth full, "I *have* done before."

"Well, you certainly are the modern woman, aren't you?"

"No—just a survivor."

As I cleaned my plate, I found myself telling this woman

more than I ever tell anyone. About being born in the Keys, the indebtedness that haunted my father wherever we moored our fishing boat, the brother who was killed working in a pit in Daytona; the sister who OD'd in Savannah; and finally, my mother going out for a pack of cigarettes and never coming home. I was so hungry that I finished whatever was left in the pots and pans on the stove. By dessert I was telling Mrs. Tudor about a drunken father who never abused me, but who fell overboard and drowned. And about the pirates who had boarded our boat.

Their "Ahoy theres" woke me up. I was lucky there had been only two of them. I stabbed the first one in the back with a galley knife when he turned around to tell the other guy that there was a young thing below, and that once they'd had their fill, it'd be over the side with me. When the pirate with the knife in his back stumbled topside, the second guy came below.

The bastard was smoking a cigar and bragging that he was bigger than any cigar. "Come out, girlie," he'd taunted, "and get what you've got coming, and if you're real nice, I'll make it quick and easy."

I'd put the propane on and climbed out the forward hatch. The bastard blew himself up the stairs and out the pilothouse.

I kicked both of them over the side and got the hell out of there, only to learn that this was just the beginning of my problems. Being fifteen, my next stop was a foster home, where it took only a few weeks for me to gauge my chances of becoming the next Cinderella. So I hit the streets: living by my wits and lying about my age, taking jobs guarding the beach and waiting tables during the off-season. For some reason I told Mrs. Tudor everything, even that I'd screwed up my relationship with my boyfriend because of my missing friend.

When I finished, I was in tears and had to rush into the bathroom, where I slammed the door, gripped the washbasin, and stared into the mirror. Why had I been crying? And for who? My father? My family? Or myself?

It was getting pretty frigging lonely living by myself. Sure, there was Dads, but he was spending more and more time with Peanut—the more promising guttersnipe? Damn, Chad, where are you when I need you? I'd drop this case and come running—if you'd only call.

When I returned to the kitchen I found the table had been cleared, Mrs. Tudor doing the dishes, and the parrot no longer on his roost but in a cage with a cloth over it. And my pistol missing from the tabletop.

"Where's my gun?"

"I don't think you're in any condition to be carrying a pistol, Susan."

"Mrs. Tudor, I need that pistol."

"Really, Susan—"

I moved to the sink where she worked on one of the pots with a wooden brush scrubber. "Mrs. Tudor, I don't have time for games. I'll go through this house and it won't be a pretty sight when I'm through."

"Susan, listen to me, you're in no shape—"

"No! You listen to me! I'll make the decisions about what shape I'm in."

She picked up another dish and scrubbed it. "I wouldn't let you drive home drunk. This is no different."

That didn't hit home. I do it all the time. "Mrs. Tudor, if you ever want me to come back and have dinner with you, I have to have that pistol."

She considered this as she rinsed the dish in the other side of the double sink, then placed it in the drainer, ignoring a perfectly decent dishwasher under the counter. "Let's have another cup of coffee and talk about it."

"No—let's talk about Kathy Gierek."

When we were seated at the table again, Mrs. Tudor said, "Kathy comes from an old-line labor family and it didn't please her father that his only daughter lived in a right-to-work state. I'm not saying Kathy had anything to do with politics when she first arrived—Kathy was just another child from a middle-class family who didn't want to maintain her parent's standard of living through education and hard work."

Mrs. Tudor smiled and placed her arms on the dining table. "I guess you can see I'm too outspoken to have my children around, unless I offer them a place at the beach. That's why I haven't returned to Greenville. There my children could ignore me with impunity." She gestured toward the rear of the trailer. "There's a master bedroom back there with two sets of bunk beds I don't use. I use the smaller room. It's easier to clean and my children know the other room's always empty. There are three of them—my children, that is—and all of I ask is that they don't all come at once. I can manage having only one family at a time."

"And Kathy Gierek?"

Mrs. Tudor smiled again. "We old people do have a tendency to ramble, don't we?"

To that I said nothing.

"Kathy was enrolled at Kent State, but after another semester of poor grades she decided to remain here after spring break. Her parents were not pleased, but Kathy was of age, and like most of these children without a steady job, she almost starved to death trying to make ends meet during the off-season. I met Kathy in a convenience store. She worked the night shift so she could . . . slip out into the parking lot and . . . ."

"Turn tricks?"

"Er—yes." Tudor's cheeks reddened. "One night Kathy . . . tricked for the wrong man and he beat her so badly that she ended up in the hospital. She called me when no one else would come." Tudor smiled. "I had to be the last person in the world she thought of." After a sip of coffee, she added, "I paid Kathy's bills and had her released, then hired some boys to move her out of that tiny little apartment she shared with three other girls."

"Prostitutes?"

"Yes. It took almost a month before Kathy was in shape enough to look for another job, and I have to admit I tried to talk some sense into her while she was convalescing. I told her if she was attractive enough for men to *pay* to be with her, she should try to find work in a restaurant, at least be a waitress and let her personality work for her. It might not pay as well, but she could face herself in the mirror every morning. And Kathy did have personality, one very much like her father's. Mr. Gierek had been a successful labor organizer during the sixties." Tudor chuckled. "None of this turned out the way I intended. I built up Kathy's self-esteem to the point where she could dance topless."

"I'm sure it wasn't a straight line progression."

"Oh, no. It's just that Kathy was so down on herself when I brought her home, I thought she might take her life." With another smile, she asked, "You know how I kept her from doing that?"

I shook my head.

"I told her that she could see how important this house was to me so that if she *did* kill herself, not to do it in my home. I couldn't live in a place where someone had killed herself, especially someone who was such a fine friend."

"Looks like it worked: restoring Kathy's self-esteem, that is."

"It kept me up at night, walking the floor, when she didn't come home."

"At least you saved her long enough to get her involved in her father's line of work. That must've felt rewarding."

"I think that was more Kathy growing up than anything I said. I counseled her to make up with her parents, but that took time. After all, her father was as hostile as any father to the idea of this daughter taking off her clothes in front of strangers. Did you know that Kathy makes over fifty thousand dollars a year dancing in the . . . nude?"

"Then why strike? It's like killing the golden goose."

"Kathy finally started taking responsibility for her life and others, including your friend, Nancy Noel."

"What were their demands?"

"Mr. Flaxx wouldn't pay for the dancers' health insurance, and Kathy said most businesses paid their employees' health benefits."

I pushed back from the table and took a cigarette from my fanny pack. A cup of coffee after a good meal can only do so much. "Let me guess. Flaxx said the dancers were in business for themselves and had to provide their own health benefits?"

"Yes, yes, that's right."

I looked around but found no ashtray. I looked at Tudor. No help there. I put the cigarette away. "Er—that the dancers were like any itinerant performer. The fact that they worked at his place didn't mean they were employed by him. But why did Kathy think she had Flaxx over the barrel— that he'd finally give in?"

"Mr. Flaxx charges each girl a fee for using the facilities. Kathy reasoned that some of that money had to pay for worker's comp."

"Were the girls ever threatened?"

"Mr. Flaxx said they would be blackballed along the Grand Strand. There were no actual threats of physical harm—by him."

"By him?"

"There's a bouncer who works there . . . I forget his name."

"Harold—yes, I've met him."

"Have you talked with Mr. Flaxx?"

"I'm going back later tonight. What was this about being blackballed—how could he? Those girls are free to come and go, especially if what Flaxx says about them being self-employed is true."

"I think he meant they wouldn't be able to get a job along the Grand Strand. The Open Blouse isn't the only topless bar, but the owners must pass along information about troublemakers, and Kathy would have fallen into that category."

"How were they doing—the strikers, I mean?"

"Not well at first. Then Kathy's father came up with the

slogan "Union dancers are clean dancers," and that affected Flaxx's traffic. There's something about girls being dirty that no man wants to think about."

"And it would fit with a demand for health insurance. So what do you think, that Kathy actually gave up the good fight and left town?"

"Not without saying good-bye, she wouldn't've."

"Did she have a boyfriend?"

"Larry Joyner. His father owns a painting contracting business that spruces up condos for resale."

"Were Kathy and Larry serious?" Like Chad Rivers had once been about me? God, it hurt even to think about it.

Tudor nodded. "She brought him over once to meet me. He appeared to be a clean-cut young man."

"And if I find that Kathy's gone and Larry's still here?"

A frown appeared on the old woman's face. "Then I would hope that you could pick up the phone, call Chicago, and find out that Kathy is there now."

6

Before leaving Mrs. Tudor's place, I worked the phone to come up with someone who knew Larry Joyner, the condo painter and boyfriend of Kathy Gierek. The call that paid off was the fourth Joyner listed in the telephone book.

"Larry's in Atlanta at the Braves' games," said his mother. "They had a home stand against the Cubs he didn't want to miss. You can call him next week when he returns."

"Do you have a number for him there?"

"Why would I? He's a grown man."

"Mrs. Joyner, do you know who he's with—in Atlanta?"

"Now why would he tell me? I'm only his mother." She hung up on me.

I put down the phone and flashed a weak smile at my hostess, who was pouring yet another cup of coffee for me. The phone call had hit a little too close to home—like what I received whenever I called Chad's house. Which meant it was time to do anything other than think about *that*.

I arrived at the Open Blouse just after nine and the cooler temperatures that the rain had brought were still with us.

The place was all lit up and going strong: the Stones rocking and rolling, a packed parking lot, and girls helping men through the V. There was no one walking the picket line, and just as I had that thought, a young woman in a plastic raincoat leaped out of a sedan parked across the street and ran across the highway to her post. That made sense. No way was the Open Blouse going to allow the strikers to park on their property.

The rain was still coming down and the girl's feet were certainly soaked by the time she dodged a couple of cars and reached the tarp along the curb. In this age of multimillion-dollar lawsuits who would be responsible for damages if a striker was run down crossing the street?

The woman shook off the rain, threw back the hood of her plastic raincoat, and looked around. Seeing the tarp flapping at one corner, she fastened the pole's hook back into the corner, tightened the support rope, picked up the sign, and then turned to face the approaching traffic.

Lollie Lloyd filling yet another shift. But hadn't she said there were always two strikers on duty after dark? Now that's something I would be concerned about—more than being run down by any damn car. After checking my fanny pack, I stepped down from my jeep . . . and into a puddle of water.

I leaped back into the jeep and shook off my foot.

Dammit! This was a special pair of running shoes I'd put on in honor of Harold the Bouncer. When a girl goes up against that much muscle, she needs some sort of equalizer: shoes with steel toes. I pulled my jacket tight and hustled over to the doorway of the Open Blouse.

A different set of girls barred my way when I tried to go inside, and we had to go through the wife-looking-for-the-wayward-husband-business once more before Harold was called to the door to tell me, again, I would have to come back in the morning. I wasn't interested in this shit, but that might've been my wet feet talking. Telling me to get lost, Harold had to raise his voice over ZZ Top wailing about how much women appreciate a sharp-dressed man.

Color Me Gone

"Harold," I asked, raising my voice and gesturing to the hallway as if I wanted only to come in out of the rain, "can I speak to you in confidence?"

The bouncer motioned me inside and over to one side of the hallway. "Make it quick." He glanced at the girls taking the arms of a young guy who looked like he wouldn't have any trouble finding a real date—he was that damn cute—and assisting him through the V. Oh well, even Charlie Sheen is known for using an escort service.

Harold had posted himself between me and the entrance to the lounge, which was at the end of a long hallway ending in bright lights and the sight of a girl slinging herself around on a brass pole. The hallway was adorned with pictures like those found over saloon bars in the Old West—buxom ladies with lots of white skin. Maybe it was supposed to add a sense of history to the place, perhaps even ambience.

"Listen, lady," said the bouncer, "I can't be away from the door too long. You never know when some weirdo's gonna come through that door."

"Yes," I said, ripping down the velcro of my fanny pack so my small pistol tumbled into my hand. "Like me. I'd like to see Mr. Flaxx. Now."

He did a double-take at my gun. Who knows, maybe his weapon didn't have such a lengthy barrel. "What the hell you think you're doing?"

"Harold, it's been a long day and I have a friend I'm very worried about." I stepped back. "Get those hands up. I know how to use this thing."

"But you can't come in here and pull a gun."

With a smile, I asked, "What you going to do about it—take me to see Mr. Flaxx?"

He glanced in the direction of the music. "Flaxx ain't gonna like this."

"Well, as the song goes, we don't always get what we want."

He was making up his mind as to what to do when I poked the barrel of the Smith & Wesson into his fat stomach. Now his hands went up. "Listen, Harold, I want to see Flaxx, and the longer I have to stand around and wait, the itchier my trigger finger becomes." Glancing down the hallway, I said, "And I don't want to see Flaxx on the floor."

"But I ain't supposed to take anyone upstairs."

Another jab of the pistol. "Harold, do you want to shit in a plastic bag the rest of your life?"

"Okay, okay." He nodded rapidly. "They don't pay me enough to take a bullet."

He touched a spot on the wall near a picture. The picture showed the back of a naked woman, her head turned to smile and let the boys know it'd be more fun if they could see her from the other side. This was some place—which must mean I was beginning to pick up on the ambience.

At the touch of the hidden button, a pocket door slid back, revealing dimly lit wrought iron stairs winding upward. Harold stepped inside the stairwell and I followed him, after checking either side of the door. I don't hold my weapon in the two-handed style they use on TV, but down along my side where nobody can take it away from me. Seeing nothing on either side, I stepped quickly into the room, and at all times kept my pistol trained on the bouncer.

Harold touched another button on the far wall and the pocket door slid closed in the faces of two guys who thought *this* was the route to Shangri-La. "Down the hall," he said, before the door shut the customers off from us.

I followed him up the steps. Not only did Harold have thick shoulders, he also had a very large butt. To guide myself along, I slid my free hand up the twisting railing and felt my way along, one slow step at a time. My grip tightened on the Smith & Wesson as I found myself taking shorter breaths—just like Harold. The hair on the back of my neck stood at attention. Not a good sign.

Mounted in the ceiling of the second floor hallway was a row of tiny spotlights that illuminated small pieces of sculpture in several recessed openings. It didn't take more than a glance to tell the figurines were in positions from that old and very knowledgeable textbook, the *Kamasutra*.

Color Me Gone

As I followed Harold through another pocket door that revealed an even smaller room, I asked, "I understand sex sells, and you need it plastered all over downstairs, but up here, too?"

By that time Harold was on the far side of the small room where another pocket door slid back automatically.

I scanned the tiny room; its walls dull and bare, some sort of anteroom before you reached an office I saw through the next pocket door that Harold was entering. "This is certainly a change in the ambience."

"And as far . . . as you go." The pocket door closed on Harold's heels and shut with a hiss.

The door behind me also hissed to a close, and I was left with my pistol and no one to impress.

I looked around and then up. The room was ten by ten with no lighting and absolutely nothing on the walls. Rain hit a plexiglas skylight and drowned out any sound of music from the lounge.

Through a hidden speaker above my head, I heard Harold catch his breath as he said, "Stay right where you are . . . lady. We have a special way . . . of dealing with people like you."

I stood in the dark with an overwhelming sense of having made a complete fool of myself. Not to mention that I was probably about to learn what had happened to Nancy Noel.

Keeping my pistol at the ready, I took a penlight from my fanny pack and walked over to where the bouncer had disappeared. I could feel seams in the pocket door, but I couldn't get my fingers into them. I took my Swiss army knife out and ran the longest blade up and down one of the seams, but nothing gave. The walls were not sheetrock but solid wood. The sliding panels of the pocket doors were also solid wood. I could tell when I kicked one.

I walked over to where I had first entered this small room and examined the other door. The damnable thing was hard to find even with the light. Finally, I found the seam, but there was little I could do other than run my blade up and down it. The blade never met a hinge or locking mechanism. Damn. This was just the sort of thing that happens to me when my sense of dignity has been offended.

It reminded me of the times I'd screwed up playing volleyball against girls in the sand court behind a local bar. Natalie, my doubles partner, was able to talk me into doing shit like that because I always needed the money.

"Keep your eye on the ball, Susan. The winner gets five hundred bucks."

Dusting off the sand where I'd taken a tumble, I glanced at the stands filled with guys gawking at us in our two-piece swimsuits. "I don't like being a piece of meat."

"If it's good enough for Gabrielle Reece, it's good enough for me."

"Then Gabby Reece is a whore."

"Gabby Reece has a book out. Do you have a book out, Susan?"

"I've been thinking about writing one—about my life at the beach."

Natalie had laughed. "Yeah, but who'd want to read a book about a slacker with such an attitude."

Taking a seat on the floor of my tiny prison, I pulled off my wet running shoes. Using the knife, I sliced off the rubber toe of each shoe, leaving a tiny opening in the metal beveling that formed the toe. Digging around inside my pack, I came up with the business end of a pair of matching gaffs. They look like screws with pointed heads. Leaving one in my lap, I took the threaded end of the first gaff and screwed it into the beveled end of the metal toe of the running shoe. Protecting my thumb and finger with the hem of my running suit, I tightened the pointed piece into the metal nose with my thumb and forefinger. Then I did the second shoe the same way, all the while holding the penlight in my teeth.

To test the points, I stood up and flexed my toes, rising on them until the ends snagged the wooden floor. Satisfied,

Color Me Gone

I took a whistle from my fanny pack and unclipped its lanyard, clipping the lanyard to the trigger guard of my Smith & Wesson before hanging the cord around my neck. Now, with the Swiss army knife and a bandanna stuck in my belt, I was ready to scale the wall—thanks to plenty of hard work on the practice wall at Broadway at the Beach.

Grasping the Swiss army knife, I raised my right foot and kicked one gaff-toed shoe into the wooden surface about a foot from the floor. Then I reached over my head with the knife and jammed the blade into the wood near the corner. Using the knife to hold my upper weight in the corner, I was able to pull myself up on the toe of the first shoe, then plant the other toe in the wall a foot above the first. One step at a time, I reached overhead and planted the knife, then used the gaffs as stepping stones to claw my way up the corner.

The pressure on my toes was enormous—the pain ran all the way to my ankles—and I had to grip the knife with both hands to lift my hundred and some odd pounds up the surface with only the three points to displace my weight. Hopefully, I wouldn't have to be at this too long. I leaned into the corner, wished there was something I could get my teeth into to give my toes a break, and continued to climb. Kicking one foot after another into the solid wood of the wall, I edged up the corner.

The staccato of rain on the plexiglas made it impossible to hear if anyone had entered the room below. I finally got my fingers on a ledge where the lip of the plexiglas did not quite meet the shaft. I left my knife in the wood and held onto that ledge with my fingertips, releasing some of the pressure on my toes. They gave ten little cheers.

In my precarious position, I really didn't have the patience to feel around for a way to release the plexiglas or attain the leverage to smash my way through. I simply held my pistol where I could fire point-blank overhead. Clinging to that one-inch ledge, I bent my head down and fired once, twice. The gunfire in the small, contained area was deafening. I was sure someone would hear me; then I remembered the volume of the music at the Open Blouse. Moving the barrel around, I emptied all but one round into the glass. After that I dropped my pistol to the end of the lanyard and pushed my shoulders through the shattered plexiglas.

The rain was in my face, and pieces of broken plastic tumbled off my shoulders and fell to the floor of the room. I whipped the bandanna around my hand so I could grasp the jagged edge—I didn't want to slip and fall and have to start all over again—and bent back the wet plexiglas, breaking the edges out of my way. That done, I pulled myself up with one hand, the gaffs holding from the other end, and my toes, once again, were happy to have the assistance.

On the roof I rolled to one side, brought up my pistol, and looked around. No one up here. I scrambled out of a puddle and hustled over behind an air conditioning unit. There I caught my breath as I reloaded the Smith & Wesson. Then I unscrewed the gaffs from my toes and put them and the knife back into my fanny pack. After velcroing the weapon into the pack, I stood up and walked around the roof until I found the fire escape. I was eagerly anticipating a return engagement with Harold the Bouncer.

7

I shook down my rain gear before rounding the corner to the front of the building. The next time a group of men stepped through the V, I was right behind them—the girls at the door had their hands full—then bullied my way over to where Harold stood.

He saw me coming and his mouth fell open. Without preamble I kicked him in the shin with the beveled metal toe of my running shoe. He howled, bent over, and when he looked up it was into the barrel of my Smith & Wesson. The customers didn't seem to notice. Oh, well, by the time they got inside this place, these guys were thinking with their little heads.

"Now, Harold, let's go see Mr. Flaxx, and if you give me any more shit, I won't hesitate to use this."

Grabbing his shoulder with my left hand—he was still bent over from my kick—I turned him around. Reaching under his jacket, I grabbed his cummerbund and marched him down the hallway and into the lounge.

The place was rocking. Three stages with girls in various stages of undress, two girls already topless and providing what every red-blooded American boy wants: a look at some really big tits. Two of the girls were narrow-faced and thin-framed, which accentuated the size of their augmented breasts. The other girl was moon-faced with a stomach that could use some work at the gym.

The room was as big as a church, and where the altar would have stood was the main stage on which the moon-faced girl danced. Flanking her were the two other stages with the other—er, performers. Chairs ringed each stage in semicircles, and the men in the audience waved money for the girl who would come over and offer a crevice or G-string to stick the bills into.

Along the back wall ran a fully equipped bar, behind which beefy bartenders served patrons and stuffed the larger bills into a pneumatic tube that ran upstairs. Around the room at eye level were painted murals of women walking like an Egyptian. Above them were portieres with women dancing without any clothes on. They weren't real but projected shadows tightly focused against curtains inside false doorways.

The moon-faced girl was performing a routine in which she wore a half-ass business suit and horn-rimmed glasses, blond hair tied back in a bun, and carried a leather briefcase. She appeared to be reluctantly taking off her clothes to the male chant of "Take it off, bitch! Take it off!"

Is this what turns men on? If so, women like me have a long way to go.

I pulled Harold to one side of the partition at the end of the hallway. Leaning into his ear, I said, "Harold, I want you to catch someone's eye who'll bring Flaxx over here—and remember, this stuff on stage doesn't do anything for me—my attention is on you and only you."

With the Smith & Wesson in his back, Harold stood rigid, hands at his sides, then cleared his throat and shouted to make himself heard over the audience's hoots and yells.

No one paid us the least bit of attention. The room was jammed with guys staring at the girls on the three stages; booths along the walls were occupied by girls in men's laps doing the dry hump. Most girls wore the least little thing to cover their crotch, and in that tiny garment the customers stuck their money. The sad part was I could see Nancy having the time of her life and thinking the whole scene great fun.

"Harold, I'm telling you—get Flaxx over here. Use that radio of yours if you have to."

"Okay, okay, but I'm going to have to take it off my hip."

"Do it very easy. Very easy." And to send the message, I jammed the barrel into the small of his back and held him tighter by his cummerbund.

I checked my backside as Harold unhooked the radio from his hip, cleared his throat, and spoke into it, competing with a musician from the Dark Ages of rock 'n' roll singing about getting a double shot of his baby's love. The girls on stage and in the booths loved it, the music giving them an opportunity to accentuate their pelvic thrust. Finished, Harold put away the radio.

A girl in a sheer pink top and pink underpants rushed over to Harold. Her boobs were too large to be covered by the tray she carried. "Yes, Mr. Rumfelt," she said with a nervous smile.

"Mr. Flaxx. I need to see him. Hurry!"

As the girl peered around the bouncer, I kept the pistol tight against the Harold's back and leaned into the wall so no one could sneak up from behind. "It's a problem at the front door," I explained in a normal tone of voice, which sounded like a whisper because of all the racket.

"It's a problem . . . at the front door," repeated Harold.

The girl nodded, shot a look at me, and hurried off in search of Daryl Flaxx.

We waited there with my back against the wall and one of my hands gripping the cummerbund, my other holding my pistol—when two huge guys wandered over. These guys also wore tuxes and had the same thick necks and huge arms as Harold. One of them was a black guy, the other, Arab or some other Middle Easterner.

Pulling tight on his cummerbund, I said, "Harold, I can't believe you'd be this stupid."

"I . . . I didn't call them . . . God's truth."

My eyes glanced up and down the hallway. Nothing but horny customers in a hurry to make the show. "Tell them to get lost or I'll make a mess of your cummerbund."

"Get away from me!" shouted Harold, using his hands to motion the two away. "She's got a gun."

The guys stopped and looked at me but didn't appear impressed. The black guy spoke into his radio. The Arab-looking guy studied me. Could this be the camel jockey who, according to Nancy's neighbor, had made my friend disappear?

"Harold, I'm getting a bad feeling about this."

"Please . . ." whined the big man, his huge legs sagging and pulling me down with him.

"Harold!" I jerked up on his cummerbund. "You stay on your feet or I'm going to blow your head off by accident."

His legs immediately straightenend. "Please get away . . . She's a fucking weirdo. I had her locked up, but somehow she got out. Please get away . . . ."

The two men glanced at each other, nodded, and took mercy on a man they would never look at in quite the same way. They backed up and positioned themselves less than ten feet away.

"You know, bitch, if you didn't have that pistol, I'd fix your ass good."

"Harold, do you know the number of guys who've said that and have never come even close?" Well, one had, but Harold didn't have to know about that.

"How—how did you get out?"

"That's for me to know and for you to clean up. That room's a real mess."

"But nobody . . ." His voice trailed off as an attractive, middle-aged man crossed the room. "You're in big trouble, girlie. Nobody screws with Mr. Flaxx."

"Bold talk for a man only an ill-timed remark away from having his spine severed."

Flaxx was about my height, tanned, earrings in both ears,

and long golden hair trailing over an upright collar. His brown short-sleeved shirt was worn tail-out and open at the neck, displaying a gold chain over a thick growth of chest hair. Dark, penetrating eyes distinguished him from the Neanderthal I held by the scruff of his cummerbund.

Flaxx's eyes widened when he realized someone stood behind his bouncer. "What's going on here?"

"Boss, I had her locked up—"

I jammed the Smith & Wesson into Harold's back hard enough to leave a bruise. "I'll do the talking." Over the thick-necked man's shoulder, I said, "I have a thirty-eight in Harold's back. If you don't want people to read in the paper tomorrow about the crazy woman who shot up this place, you and I will go somewhere and talk."

"Harold, how did she get in?"

"I had her locked up in the foyer, Mr. Flaxx, but she got out . . . somehow."

"'The foyer.'" I laughed. "Is that what you call that dipshit place any kid could break out of?" We had to do something. My nerves were frayed and I didn't know how much longer I could hold on before my trembling hand fired off a random shot. As a precaution, I moved my finger outside the trigger guard.

"But no one has ever . . . The cops have taken several people into custody from the . . . from that room when they came here to rob me." Flaxx gestured at the bar where plastic tubes ran up into the ceiling. "Thieves know all the money's kept upstairs."

"Sorry to ruin your plans, asshole," I said with a wild laugh, "but I need to talk with you."

"Please, boss," begged Harold. "Could you talk to her . . . somewhere?"

Flaxx stared at his bouncer for a long moment, then glanced at me again. "Okay. But you could've asked for an appointment."

"Yeah. Sure." Gesturing with my head to the left and right, I said, "Get rid of those two bozos."

To the bouncers watching our little party, he said, "I'll handle this."

"But, Mr. Flaxx," said the Arab-looking guy, reaching inside his coat, "Harold said she has a gun."

"Harold!" I shouted into his ear. "Do something here!" The big man jumped. My finger was back *inside* the trigger guard.

"Please . . ." was all he could get out.

"Flaxx, you are one dumb son of a bitch. How many mugs you think you'll be able to get to work in this place if you don't take care of this man? And I will surely shoot him if you don't call off your dogs."

"Okay, okay," said Flaxx, holding up his hands. "Just calm down." To the other two, he said, "Put the guns away and leave us alone. We're just going to talk."

"Yeah," I said, gesturing my head around the room, "and get away from this fucking noise."

"Listen, lady, just because you can't appreciate—"

"Fuck that! Let's get moving."

The other bouncers gave way as I followed Flaxx across a room—where the occupants ignored a fully dressed young woman fastened to a bouncer's back. Well, it wasn't what you came here to ogle.

We passed center stage where the men were yelling "Take it off, bitch. Take it off," to the working girl. The girl was in tears, down to her underwear, and on her knees. Then past a room where customers had been almost stripped naked and were being photographed at the mercy of some black-leathered, whip-carrying Amazon.

I glanced behind me to make sure the other two bouncers weren't tagging along, then turned to see Flaxx stop at the end of the bar. He tapped a touch pad, another pocket door slid open, and Flaxx gestured us through.

I shook my head. "No, sir. Assholes first."

Flaxx snorted, then stepped through the door, which led to another iron stairwell to the second floor. The small room had a bit more light than the previous one and held an ice machine. Liquor boxes were piled to the ceiling.

Color Me Gone

"I have to climb damn stairs again?"

"Space is at a premium along the Grand Strand, Miss . . . what is your name? You're not vice, are you?"

"Susan Chase and I'm private."

Flaxx tapped a spot on the wall and the pocket door closed behind us, shutting off the noise. Heading for the stairs, he asked, "Are you in the employ of some wife looking for a wayward husband?"

"Wish that I were. You make men take their eye off the ball."

"Don't be silly." Flaxx started up the metal stairwell. "We give those men fantasies their wives could never give them, even if they wanted to."

"And for good reason."

"Miss Chase, what we do here is simply beyond your understanding."

"Then there must be a god after all." I gripped the bodyguard's cummerbund. "Harold, I want you to climb those stairs, and as you do, remember I'll put a bullet up your ass if you give me any hint of trouble. No tricks—understand? I'm not going back in that fucking foyer."

"Gotcha."

"Flaxx?"

The boss man took his hands off the upstairs railing and held them out, open. "No tricks."

He stepped back from the stairs, and as I reached him, I saw another series of spotlights illuminating more tiny sculptures: more *Kamasutra*. This frigging place was beginning to get to me. But instead of losing my focus, I kept one hand on the bouncer's cummerbund, the other on my pistol. You could say my eyes were fixed firmly on the ball.

8

Ahead of us was another room similar to the foyer where I'd been held captive. From where I stood I figured we were just around the corner. Below us thumped the sound of a disco beat.

Still gripping Harold's cummerbund, I said, "Okay, Flaxx, how're we going to do this?"

From inside the small room, Flaxx said, "Just come through the door, Miss Chase."

I shook my head. "I don't want to have to climb out of another of your damn holes."

"Climb out . . . ?"

"You think I went out through the wall? I'm not Superman, just Supergirl. Now, if you'll back over here to the door and raise the tail of your shirt, you can exchange places with Harold."

"Look, lady, I really don't think—"

"I don't give a damn what you think!"

Harold flinched. "I wish you'd do . . . what she's asking . . . Mr. Flaxx." Harold was having a hard time catching his breath after another climb up those stairs. Or perhaps it had something to do with the barrel of my pistol bruising his spine.

Flaxx came out of the foyer, turning his back to me and raising the tail of his shirt.

"Use both hands," I said. "And keep the tail of the shirt up where I can grab hold of the belt."

"These pants don't take a belt."

"You know what the hell I'm talking about!" I was in my hysterical-girl mode now. Men seem to respond. Or run and hide.

Flaxx sighed, then did as I asked so I could get my hand on his Sansabelt. I shoved Harold down the dimly lit hallway and grabbed the back of his boss's pants. As the bouncer stumbled away, his hand moved to the front of his jacket.

"Watch it, Harold!" I said, jamming my pistol against the back of Flaxx's neck. "By now I'd think you know I have a low tolerance for stupidity."

"Don't worry," said Flaxx, calmly raising his hands. "I can take it from here."

The bouncer nodded and I kept my pistol trained on him as he retreated down the wrought iron circular stairs. The look on his face warned me not to find myself in any dark alleys with him—or locked up in small rooms.

After the door below us had slid open and then shut, I said to my hostage, "You and I are going through that room together, Mr. Flaxx. One wrong move and I'm going to shoot you. It might be a clean hit or it might be a bit messy, but at this point I don't give a damn. Got that?"

"I understand, though you don't have to be so melodramatic."

"Shut the hell up!" I said, jerking on his pants. "I'm the one with the pistol so I can be any damn way I please. Now get moving."

We went though the foyer without any trouble, Flaxx punching the touch pad and the panel sliding back to admit us into his office. This time I was inside before the panel closed behind me. Once in the office I pushed Flaxx away and backed up to the wall so I could scope out the place.

Steve Brown

The private office of Daryl Flaxx was quite a contrast to the raucous lounge and darkened hallways we'd left behind. You could've been in the office of one of the Fortune 500. It was spacious, about thirty-feet square, with thick wine-red carpeting. The walls and ceiling were painted a soft gray. Color lithographs of Degas ballet dancers graced the walls, well lit by lamps on the corners of mahogany furniture. In the center of the room was a broad mahogany desk with a high-backed chair. On the desk, a humidor, a silver lighter, and a ceramic ashtray. Two straight-backed chairs waited for visitors. Against one wall, flanked by more straight-backed chairs, stood a table displaying magazines in neat rows and a vase of freshly cut hibiscus.

The air was fresh and cool and held a fragrance I couldn't identify. None of the noise and bedlam reached us from the downstairs lounge, but you could see everything there. Six nineteen-inch TV screens were mounted on the wall adjacent to the door, four more behind my back. Three of the six showed the showroom as cameras panned the room: girls dancing on stage or wrestling with customers at their own private tables. There was even a camera for the room with the whip-toting Amazon and her prey. The young woman who had once been dressed as a business executive now begged for mercy in her underwear. The screens in the "foyers" also had cameras. In one you could see where the plexiglas lay in pieces on the floor. The final screen featured the V at the front door. I'd never noticed a camera. I'd been too worried about getting out of the rain, and that hadn't been very professional of me.

Flaxx was staring at one of the monitors. "You smashed the plexiglas and went out through the roof?"

"Seemed like the thing to do." I remembered my tenuous hold where the plexiglas had not come flush with the frame. I flexed that hand. My fingers still ached, but with all the excitement, I hadn't noticed. My toes were still sore.

"But that ceiling's over twenty feet high—so men can't stand on each other's shoulders and climb out."

"What can I say?" I shrugged. "Little Alice grew."

He went around his desk. "Well, if you're here to rob me, I don't think that's going to work. I'm sure Harold is now calling the police."

"From what I've seen I don't think you operate that way. You've got something to hide, Flaxx, and I'm going to find out what it is." I crossed the room to the chairs in front of his desk.

"Now what would that be?"

"We'll get into that once you've come out from behind that desk."

"What?"

"I don't want any more tricks."

"You want to know where the money's kept." He stared at me. "But a girl . . . I never thought a girl would rob me."

"Why's that? You employ plenty."

"Yes, but . . . ."

"Move it, asshole. Your lack of sensitivity is beginning to irritate me."

He moved from behind the desk to one of the chairs, and I leaned against the desk and kept the pistol trained on him. "The garbage you have to go through to get a few answers. I probably won't believe anything you say and end up hanging around forever. The strikers won't be your only problem."

"What's your scam, Chase?"

"I want information."

"Information about what?"

"Nancy Noel."

"Nancy Noel? What do you want with that dumb broad?"

"She may be a dumb broad to you, but she's a friend of mine and her son's worried about her."

"Oh, yeah, right." Flaxx sat back in the chair and glanced at the humidor on the corner of the desk. "When he's not looking down his nose at how his mother earns her money." He reached for the humidor. "I suppose you also sympathize with those girls on the picket line." After taking out a cigar, he gave me the once-over. "Take off those warm-ups so I can see what you've got."

I really didn't know what to say to that.

"Most girls with shoulders like yours run to fat. I want to see your tits."

Rolling off the desk, I said, "I came here for answers, not looking for a job."

"How much do you make as a private eye?" He clipped off the end of the cigar. "It can't be much. A job where you get the shaft more than adequate compensation."

"Right on both accounts, but why'd you think I'd want to work in a place like this?"

"Because I've revolutionized the skin trade along the Grand Strand, and it had to be done to compete with the Internet. Anyone with a little knowledge of HTML can set up his own web site, whether it's live on a web cam or a bunch of old photographs of his wife. And the cops know there's nothing illegal going on and leave me alone, unless some church group makes them send someone in undercover. I hire them, the cops I mean. I hire all of them. That surprises you. Some female cops have nice bodies."

"You really have an attitude, don't you?"

He shook his head, then took the silver lighter off the desk and lit up. "You're not interested in earning up to fifty thousand dollars in eight to nine months?"

"Not the way you suggest."

"Oh, you have ties to the community? A family? You don't have to live here forever. Save half of what you make over the next ten years and you can live in style the rest of your life—here or in Florida. Or California."

A breath of smoke headed in my direction. I did not cough. I'd smoked cigars before.

"Four of my girls are in Coastal Carolina, one is working on her master's. She plans to return to Alabama and be a marine biologist. Now, how many people in Alabama are likely to recognize her—a girl who stripped along the Grand Strand? You should consider it."

"I would think most of your girls come from disadvantaged backgrounds."

Color Me Gone

"One of the usual misconceptions, though many do." His mouth formed a ring of smoke that hung in the air between us. "But some are in it strictly for the money. I have no idea if they're turning tricks on the side, but anyone found blowing a customer is out the door, and very quickly, too."

I gestured at the room with my pistol. "You're telling me that men's fantasies fuel all this, that you don't have another angle?"

Flaxx shifted around in his chair. "Is it possible that you might put the gun away? You're making me nervous."

I considered this, then backed across the room and returned the Smith & Wesson to my fanny pack. His eyebrows went up as the gun was velcroed into the fanny pack on my hip.

"Pretty slick."

"I like to think so. Now stretch out your legs and cross your ankles or it comes out again."

He smiled, stretched his legs, and crossed his ankles. "You really think women have the energy, or the inclination, after a day's work to get a rise out of their husbands? It's the last thing they're interested in. So the guys stop by here to get their engines racing. Then they go home and finish business, whether the wife participates or not."

"I never thought men needed all that much to get their engines racing."

Flaxx eyed the cigar like he would an attractive woman. "Then you're dating some rather simple fucks. Husbands may not know much about romance, but their wives have forgotten everything about sex—unless they are the girls who work for me."

"Women—if they're that clever."

"Girls if you want to turn a man on. Men are afraid of women."

"And Nancy Noel?"

"Perfect for the job. She just wanted to dance, peel off her clothes, and take home a large paycheck. Not a lot of brainpower there so she was easy to manage, until she got mixed up with the damn strike."

"All the strikers wanted was health insurance."

He pulled his legs under the chair as he sat up. "The rates are astronomical for dancers. The insurance companies think they're all whores."

"Why didn't you simply split the cost of insurance with them?"

"What's in it for me?"

I gestured around the large room. "There have to be enough problems running a place like this that you don't need any more."

Flaxx shifted around in his chair, then remembered to straighten out his legs. "I'm not going to coddle anyone who can make fifty thousand dollars in six months and might leave anytime they want for a so-called better offer across the street." He took another drag off the cigar and let out another small "O" of smoke. "These girls don't have any loyalty—until they've worked down the street and come crawling back. My retention rate of those who've tried other places is eighty percent, while on the other hand, most who leave my employment are pregnant. I'm supposed to offer pregnancy benefits to some girl who gets knocked up, maybe even broke one of my rules about screwing the customers?" He shook his cigar in my direction and a small bit of ash fell to the carpeted floor. "Two of those five will get pregnant and I'll have to pay."

"So exclude pregnancy."

He shook his head. "The image of these girls is: Ten minutes in the parking lot is better than an hour on stage. No insurance company is going to touch that kind of employee."

All this garbage was beginning to bore me. "What happened to Nancy Noel?"

"After she was kicked out, she ended up on the picket line. After that I don't care."

"She's disappeared and her son's worried about her."

"Like I said, you want to find Nancy, okay, but don't come in here blowing smoke about Sammy Noel giving a damn about his mother. Nancy complains the boy spends too much time with some old fart who has a schooner moored along the Intracoastal. If you're so worried about Sammy maybe you should check out that guy."

That was Dads he was slandering. "I already have."

"Checked her house? She could be sick."

"I've already been there. The neighbors said she left town with a boyfriend."

"Well, then, there it is, and when Nancy wants to come home, she will. I know these girls, Chase. They get a little ahead and the money burns a hole in their pocket. They want to have a good time and head to Atlanta on a shopping spree. Nancy Noel, most of all."

"I thought all your girls were attending Coastal Carolina, working on their master's."

"Nah, that comes later. When the first wrinkles begin to show." Flaxx took another drag off his cigar and let the smoke out gradually. "So Sammy's had his allowance cut off, sicked you on me, and now you've come up empty. What are you going to do?" He untangled his feet as if to stand. When he did, my hand moved to my fanny pack and he quickly raised his hands in surrender. "Now, now, be reasonable. I have to get back to work."

"Cross your legs like before. I'm not through with you." The pistol was in my hand now.

"Chase . . . ."

"Cross them!"

Reluctantly, he did so. "You know, I was going to let you walk out of here—no problem, but now . . . ."

"What I can't figure is why both Nancy Noel and Kathy Gierek disappeared at the same time."

Flaxx shrugged. "Not my problem."

"No—it's mine, but I'm going to keep sniffing around until I find out why two girls who walked the picket line have disappeared in the same week."

He snubbed out the cigar. "I don't have to take any more of this. I don't give a damn if you've got a pistol or not. I'm phoning the cops."

Steve Brown

Calling his bluff, I went around the desk to the credenza, picked up the phone, and placed it in front of him. "Be my guest."

"Listen," he said, leaning over and punching in some numbers, "this is your last chance. You can walk out of here with no hassle or I'm going to lodge a complaint."

I was still trying to figure his angle when the dispatcher came on the line.

With a last glance at me, Flaxx turned the instrument into a speakerphone. "No takers? Okay. Dispatch, I've got some half-assed private eye holding a pistol on me because she says I'm responsible for the disappearance of her friend."

The dispatcher was a woman. "Where is this, sir?"

"The Open Blouse near the bypass. I'm the owner, Daryl Flaxx. Could you send someone over? I'd appreciate it if it wasn't from the uniform division. It tends to upset the customers. Ask Lieutenant Halcrow. He knows me."

"Sir, Lieutenant Halcrow is not on duty tonight."

"I don't care who it is. I want this bitch out of here and I don't want you sending over a uniformed unit."

"Sir, we have procedures to follow."

"Yes, yes, I'm sure you do, and because you're a woman, you'll make sure they have their lights flashing." Before he broke the connection, Flaxx said to me, "Chase, you're putting me in the mood to take that pistol away from you and make you eat it."

With a smile, I said, "Except your threat was heard over the speakerphone and now it's on tape."

Flaxx jerked his head around to the speaker and saw his finger still poised over the button.

The dispatcher for the Horry County Police said, "Sir, the lady is correct. A unit has been dispatched to your location."

"Aw, shit," muttered Flaxx.

"And, sir, if you don't want any further problems, please keep this line open."

Flaxx's hand dropped into his lap. He slumped into his chair.

"I'm surprised you didn't call your attorney first."

Now he looked up. "For what? A dipshit like you?"

Over the speakerphone the dispatcher asked, "Mr. Flaxx says you have a gun, Miss Chase. Is that true?"

"I'm licensed."

"Then you need to speak to the shift supervisor."

When he came on the line, the sergeant had the same questions. "Well, Miss Chase, you may not be licensed much longer if these charges hold up. You can't go around threatening citizens—no matter what type of license you hold" On the other end of the line, he paused. "Now I see what we're talking about. But it says you look for runaways."

"Damn." Flaxx shook his head. "I'll get even with you, Chase, if it's the last thing I do."

"Was that a threat I just heard?" asked the male voice on the other end of the speakerphone. "I must warn you . . . Mr. Flaxx, that everything is recorded."

"Damn," muttered Flaxx again, and he stared at the floor but not for long. His head jerked up. "Could they ask for Harold at the front door? He'll bring them up the back way so my customers won't be disturbed. They're mostly tourists, you know."

"We can do that," said the voice. "And, Miss Chase, what about that pistol?"

"Mr. Flaxx and I will meet your people at the back door. We're leaving now."

"And the pistol?"

"I don't want to have some kind of accident before your people arrive."

"Miss Chase, you will be under the protection of the Horry County Police Department, but you must surrender your weapon." He paused. "Our units are approaching your location. Why don't you start downstairs?"

To Flaxx, I said, "The shift supervisor sounds as if he's been here before."

"Most have," said Flaxx, getting to his feet. "We're the class act of the Grand Strand." He started for a pocket door.

I disconnected the speakerphone and followed him through the open panel and across the broken pieces of plexiglas. "You know, I never did see the room you thought I was looking for."

"And what's that?" asked Flaxx as the panel slid into the wall and opened into the darkened hallway.

"Where you keep all your money."

He gestured at the ceiling. "It's up there."

"The pneumatic tubes suck it up there?"

"Yes."

The panel slid back, revealing Harold in the dimly lit hallway. "Mr. Flaxx, there are a bunch of cops outside and I didn't call them."

"It's okay. Go on back downstairs." To me, Flaxx said, "What do you think this is—some Mickey Mouse operation? I've been robbed before, but it's never going to happen again. That's why I have these foyers."

"I don't know how many times I have to tell you, but I don't give a damn about your money. I just want to find Nancy Noel."

"And that's why I don't believe you. Nobody could be that interested in a broad as dumb as Nancy Noel."

9

Warden was waiting for me at the law enforcement center. J.D. Warden had given up the good life of the Big Apple after taking a bullet in the line of duty. Upon learning his daughter's husband would be assigned to Sumter Air Force Base—a short drive from Myrtle Beach—Warden applied for and received an appointment, at a much-reduced salary, to the South Carolina State Law Enforcement Division (SLED) Grand Strand.

SLED agents, like those of the FBI, are considered interlopers, interfering in the hodgepodge of Grand Strand fiefdoms of at least five city police departments, a county police, *and* a county sheriff's department. SLED has the authority to investigate anything and go anywhere. It has only to be asked. Sometimes it doesn't wait to be asked.

Despite my arrest occurring in the middle of a shift, there were still enough cops around to stare at me as I was dragged back to see my guardian angel.

Warden looked up from his paperwork. His jacket hung on a rack near a sign that said, "Thank you for not smoking." The gray metal desk was standard government issue.

Another desk and chair faced the wall to my left. That would be partner DeShields' desk. Mickey Dee was not there. Also missing would be any hint of compassion.

A husky man with wide shoulders, dark eyes, and skin that does not tan, J.D. Warden combs his black hair like basketball coach Pat Riley—straight back. His shirt was white on white, his tie maroon, and I didn't have to see his shoes to know he wore the obligatory wingtips. He said, "Sit," and motioned me to one of the two matching chairs in front of the desk.

"Cuffs, please." I turned my back to the sergeant who had brought me in.

The sergeant glanced at Warden, and after a nod from the other side of the desk, uncuffed me and sat me down. Why Warden thinks he's responsible for me I have no idea. I'm a big girl and can take care of myself.

As the sergeant placed my paperwork on the desk, I opened my fanny pack and took out my cigarettes. Without looking up, Warden gestured at the "No Smoking" sign. The sergeant left, closing the door behind him.

"Sorry, but smoking *is* permitted when you're incarcerated." I lit up and blew a ring across his desk.

He looked up from the paperwork. "You're not making this any easier, Chase."

"Mind telling me why I'm not locked up where I can smoke to my heart's content, call my attorney, and sue your ass for false arrest?"

"You may have to smoke, but do you also have to curse?"

"Matter of fact, I do. This is the second time I've been rousted today."

"And probably for good reason."

"I'm sure that's what you'd like to think." I continued to puff away on my smoke.

"Tell me all about it," he said, putting down the paperwork. "Tell me how everyone's picking on you and you have no other choice but to be a horse's ass."

So I told him about the cops rousting me at Nancy Noel's house.

He picked up another form and read it. "It appears they were only doing their job."

I followed that with being locked in a frigging closet at the Open Blouse, then handcuffed and brought downtown.

"An owner defending his property, and that closet, as you call it, has been responsible for catching two sets of thieves. Whether I approve of how the man makes his living or not, he has a right to defend his property."

"No telling what else goes on in there."

Warden sighed. "Chase, I'm going home, but I can arrange for you to spend the night here, smoking those cigarettes. Do you want to tell me what your problem is—this time?"

"I want to know where Nancy Noel is."

He glanced at the form he had retrieved from the "out" tray. "Says here she left town with her boyfriend. Before I had them bring you back, I checked with Missing Persons to be sure. There is no Jane Doe in the county morgue, or any of the hospitals, except a brunette fished from the river two nights ago. That help?"

"Nancy Noel didn't have a boyfriend. Nobody will hang with her long enough to qualify."

A smile crossed Warden's face. "That's what they say about you, but every once in a while you surprise us. This young man, Chad Rivers, now that's trolling in rather rich waters, isn't it?"

I shrugged.

"You fail to connect with him and you'll be making a big mistake. Chad Rivers isn't some musician or tourist passing through."

"No—he's a frigging playboy."

"So that's what's bothering you—that someone might be running a game on you. It's been done before. Like tonight. Now are you going to stay away from the Open Blouse or would you rather spend the night at the county's expense?"

I sat up. "Not only is Nancy Noel missing, but so is her friend Kathy Gierek, the person leading the strike."

Warden glanced at the report again. "It's all here. What's the problem? People in that line of work come and go. We're not talking about a regular job."

I leaned forward. "Dammit, J.D., she makes fifty grand a year. That's about as regular as you can get."

"For taking off her clothes in public."

I sat back in my chair. "Nancy owned a house, had a son, and a cat, too."

"I have a dog, but he doesn't keep me from going on vacation—as your friend may have done."

"You don't take vacations."

"It couldn't be coincidental that these two girls left town at the same time?"

"Women, please."

He shrugged.

"Nancy would've told me if she was going away."

"Yes, Chase, I'm sure you're at the center of a good number of people's universe."

"Yours for sure."

"Cut the crap. What are you saying—about these women's disappearance?"

"If they moved, did they leave forwarding addresses?"

Warden considered this, then picked up the phone on the credenza behind him. "I'm going to check this, but if there is a forwarding address, I want your word you'll back off and leave Daryl Flaxx alone. They already have enough problems with this strike."

"I don't know why you're protecting those scumbags. The county council has tried to zone them out of existence. Anyway, why would Kathy Gierek leave the strike she started? She comes from an old labor family."

"Women do the strangest things when they're in love. That's why I'm hoping someday you find a guy and settle down—so I can get some peace and quiet." As he punched numbers into his phone, he added, "You modern women pass up a good number of men because of your newfound arrogance."

I had a pretty decent comeback, but Warden waved me off as someone came on the other end of the line. Even though it was after hours, Warden exercised his authority with the post office. Some postal worker went looking for Noel's and Gierek's forwarding addresses.

He waited and I waited. I thought about smoking another cigarette, then thought better of it.

"Thank you," he said, hanging up. "Well, Chase, I guess you're out of the private eye-business."

I gritted my teeth. "So that's what this is all about."

"Kathy Gierek's forwarding address is her parents' home near Chicago. Noel's is Ravenwood Academy, that exclusive boy's school in Georgetown."

"That's her son's address, J.D."

"But good enough to send you back to lifeguarding. And if I remember correctly, you stated on your PI's application that you'd look for runaways, not get involved in domestic cases."

"You vouched for me."

"That I did. It clears man-hours for real police work, especially during the Season. But you're sticking your nose where it doesn't belong. And you're on probation—because of the young man who leaped to his death from the Garden City pier."

"That punk was on drugs. I wanted nothing to do with him. It was his girlfriend I was after."

"But the city still had to defend itself against the wrongful death suit brought by that boy's parents. Some people thought your license should be revoked."

"Did that include you?"

He placed his elbows on his desk. "Chase, I don't think I'm getting through. There has to be some give-and-take on each side. I went to bat for you when that boy drowned." He gestured at the phone. "And I expect you to stay away from the Open Blouse. Both women have forwarding addresses."

"What you're telling me is that you don't think there's something fishy about two girls disappearing at the same time and from the same place?"

He pointed at his empty "out" tray. "Tomorrow that will be full and I don't want to have to deal with you."

"You never had to deal with me. You could've let me sit in stir or let me make my phone call."

"Maybe next time I will."

"Why don't you?"

"Is that what you'd like—to be left in a cell with a bunch of hookers, dopers, and strippers?"

I sat back and stared at him. "You really have a problem with this sex thing, don't you?"

Warden shook a finger at me, as many have done in the past and will probably do in the future. "Hookers, dopers, strippers—all scum I have to deal with. Day in and day out. You don't have to but for some reason choose to. I know you come from poor circumstances, and I'm not talking about economic considerations. Your family was a bunch of vagabonds but that's no reason for you not to make something of yourself. You have a lot of potential, Chase, natural ability, and brains. You could be rather attractive if you took the time to fix yourself up and do something with your hair. There's a tech school at the beach, a college that's part of the university system—things you could avail yourself of, but you choose not to. Instead you hang around people like Nancy Noel."

I was gripping the chair so I wouldn't come out of it—or perhaps so I could. "Nancy doesn't have anyone to take care of her. Her mother's dead and she hasn't seen her father in years."

"And that's your business?"

"She's my friend, J.D."

"You made her your friend." I tried to interrupt, but he waved me off. "And that's why you're having trouble with this Rivers kid. He's a step up. A step up you're afraid to take."

By now I was seething. "With the mind of a twelve-year-old and a son to raise, who's going to help Nancy do that?

Social Services? They'd put Sammy in a foster home. But Nancy found a way to take care of her kid, put him in an exclusive school, and along the way became one of those people you want me to become—a useful member of society."

"You could do more. Be someone Nancy Noel can look up to."

"Twelve-year-old girls don't look up to anyone but the latest teen idol."

"And who's your role model, Chase?"

Flashing a cheery smile, I said, "I want to be like you, J.D. I just don't want to dress like you."

"Get out of here, Chase." He waved his hand. "I've got real work to do." When I stood up, he said, "And remember our deal: You're to stay away from the Open Blouse."

"I didn't like the answer you received for Nancy Noel and I'll check out the one for Kathy Gierek."

He shook his head wearily. "You're picking up the standard for these people. Not only are they not worth it, but it makes you have to defend their cause. Admit it, Chase, you've chosen these people and you don't have the nerve to admit you've made a mistake."

"Is that why you'd like me hooked up with Chad Rivers?"

"No. Rivers has too much money. You could still mess around and get in trouble. I'd rather you marry some poor kid and have to struggle to make ends meet."

"At least that would keep me out of your hair."

He finally smiled. "And that's the general idea, Chase. That's the general idea."

10

I left the law enforcement center and returned to the Open Blouse. I might have a deal with J.D. Warden about approaching people working there, but there was no agreement about approaching those *who no longer worked there.* On my return trip, I stopped by a Waffle House. While they were fixing my sandwich, I called Skokie, Illinois, and was connected with a sister of Kathy Gierek.

"No, Miss Chase, Kathy's not here. She's in South Carolina."

"Your parents—may I speak to them?"

"Mom and Dad aren't here. They left a note that they're at the opera. I just got in from college."

Talk about coming up in the world. I wondered while working the line at GM if Mr. Gierek ever thought he'd live in such a neighborhood, or attend the opera.

"I was trying to reach your sister . . . ." I didn't know how much more I could say without causing unnecessary concern.

"If you don't mind my saying so, you sound like you're from there."

"How did you know?"

"Well, you do have somewhat of an accent. Do you have Kathy's address—there?"

"I know where she lives, but she's out of town. I have a question about the strike. I'll just have to make it up as I go along." None of that was a lie, and I have no idea why I worry about the truth so much.

"I can tell Daddy to call you when he comes in. He's retired, but he likes to stay involved in union business. Otherwise, he would've moved to Arizona like my uncle." That was followed by a small, hollow laugh.

As long as her old man didn't move to the Grand Strand. I still didn't like all the traffic. But the rain had finally stopped. I gave my name to the sister and told her I'd call her father in the morning. "By the way, is Larry Joyner still dating your sister?"

"I hope not. I mean, Kathy's had her problems, but if she thinks she can bring that redneck home, she'd better think again. Do I sound like my father? Oh, that's right, you've never met him. Well, that's the way he talks." Her voice deepened as she said, "Run off to live in a right-to-work state, dance naked in front of people, then bring home some redneck as a boyfriend . . . well, Miss Chase, you can see what I mean."

I understood. I'd had the same problem calling my boyfriend's house, and why did I still refer to Chad as my boyfriend? Evidently I'd 86-ed that relationship.

I called Warden and left word on his voice mail that Kathy Gierek's family thought she was in South Carolina. I also said I was still looking for her, but not at the Open Blouse.

Back at the strip club the midnight air was cool and fresh and a solitary figure paced back and forth, carrying a sign. I noticed only a few cars in the parking lot as I parked across the highway in the strip mall. When the picketer walked under the light, I saw it was Lollie Lloyd. I had no idea why the woman was pulling a double shift, but that wasn't my business. My business was with *whoever* pulled the last shift. So I sat in my jeep enjoying my coffee and sandwich from the Waffle House, finally getting a blanket out of a locker welded to the floorboard where a backseat should be. Snuggling in, I watched Lloyd plod back and forth.

Midnight came and went and still Lloyd trudged on, and because it was dark, the weirdos passing by gained more confidence. Vehicles would occasionally pull up beside her, the driver would say something, be shot the bird, and roar off with a squeal of rubber and a wild laugh.

Near one o'clock, the last customer was shown the door, actually helped through the V by Harold the bouncer. He stood on the steps, staring at the redhead as she trudged back and forth along her muddy trail paralleling the highway.

I sat up when he came down the stairs and watched him cross the hundred or so feet of the parking lot to where Lloyd made her turn. He said something, but she ignored him, turning on her heel and heading back down her muddy trail. Harold followed her, parts of their one-sided conversation drifting across the four-lane to me.

". . . won't have anything to do with you . . . you'd better get . . . ." that was all I heard before they headed toward the far end of the property—where Lloyd turned on the asshole and cursed him out but good. That floated across the blacktop to me on the night air. As they stood under the light, I could see Harold's face twisted up in that senseless stupidity I'd witnessed myself. Before I could throw off the blanket and leap out of my jeep, Harold snatched the sign from Lloyd's hand and tore it in half.

The redhead screamed and grabbed at him, but the big man only laughed, turning his back on her. When she tried to get around him, he moved with her, ripping the torn poster to pieces. Lloyd was left to hammer on the bouncer's back until he finished. Turning around, his hand came up. That's when I scrambled out of the jeep and reached for my fanny pack.

Color Me Gone

Okay, okay, I was already out of the jeep, the pistol dropping into my hand as I stepped into the highway. Nothing in my agreement with Warden said I had to stand around and watch men abuse women—unless they were performing on stage at the Open Blouse.

A pickup whipped by only inches from my gun hand and someone yelled at me for standing in the middle of the road. This might be a dumb move, but it had gotten Harold's attention. His hand lowered, probably thinking the yell from the pickup had been meant for him. Then he saw me in the middle of the highway.

He sneered at Lloyd, called her a few juvenile vulgarities, and stalked off, pitching the pieces of the sign into a puddle on his way back to the Open Blouse. I velcroed my pistol back into my fanny pack and returned to my jeep. After tucking my blanket in my footlocker—Lloyd was surely ready to leave—I saw she had returned to pacing back and forth in the muddy path along the highway.

What was up with that? Her sign was history, the Open Blouse was closed, and there was nothing to be gained by remaining on the job.

Fifteen minutes later a group of dancers left the building and walked to their cars. Breaking away from the group, two of the women walked over and spoke to Lloyd. Both young women wore sweats, carried gym bags, and had their hair up in scarves. Gentle laughter followed the two women as they walked away from Lloyd and joined their companions in their cars. Eventually these cars also left, disappearing down the bypass. After that, only a Cadillac, a BMW sports car, and a couple of sport utility vehicles remained. Still Lloyd continued her vigil. She held a replacement sign, albeit much smaller, but she carried that piece of poster board from the entrance of the parking lot to the corner and back again.

A few minutes later, the black bouncer and the Arab-looking fellow sauntered out of the building. They glanced in the direction of the picketer, then got into their vehicles and left.

Both men saw me sitting in my jeep across the street, smoking a cigarette and studying their place of business. The Arab-looking fellow pulled out of the parking lot, taking his time making the turn onto the bypass as if memorizing what I looked like and what kind of vehicle I drove. Then he was gone, squealing rubber. But the black man was different. He drove directly into the strip mall and stopped his car alongside mine.

"Waiting for someone?" he asked, his arm on the window and a leer on his face.

"If I was, it certainly wouldn't be you." I threw off the blanket I'd reclaimed from the footlocker and showed him the Smith & Wesson that Lt. Warden had returned to me.

His leer disappeared. "You know, one day you're gonna pull that gun on the wrong person."

"Still," I said with an easy smile, "I'm sure it'll be more impressive than any weapon of yours."

With a snarl he was gone, duplicating the squealing rubber of the Arab-looking bouncer—who in his incomparable wisdom had decided not to screw with me.

It was fifteen minutes past two when Flaxx and Harold came out and answered the question: How do you get an open blouse to close. Hey, what can I say? It was way past late, I was sleepy as hell, and there was damn little to do but consider the trivialities of life, especially Lollie Lloyd's state of mind.

While I was puzzling this out, Flaxx focused a remote on the front of the building and two barn-sized doors slid over the V, activating a red light at the top. I'd never noticed. The huge doors were painted the same as the front of the building. Heading for his car, Flaxx was met with a remark from Lloyd.

". . . playing fair . . ." was all I heard. Her back was to me. I sat up. The dummy was playing with fire.

The bouncer started in her direction until something said by Flaxx stopped him. Harold told his boss he could get rid of the bitch—that much carried across the highway. Flaxx only shrugged, then walked over to the Cadillac, got in, and drove away. As his car disappeared down the bypass, Lloyd's shoulders sagged but immediately stiffened when Harold drove by, uttering filthy noises. Once he reached the black-top, the bouncer gave me the eye before following his boss into the darkness.

The road was quiet now, except for the cicadas and a woman's sobs. While I was speculating about her relation-ship with her former boss, Lloyd wiped the tears away, fished pieces of her sign out of the puddle, and crossed the street. Using a remote of her own, she opened a Toyota sedan parked several yards from me. Before climbing in, Lloyd stared at me over the top of the car. She opened her mouth to say something, thought better of it, and then climbed into her car. When she drove away, I was right behind her.

11

We drove into town, then north along Kings Highway into North Myrtle Beach. Along the way we passed two other topless joints that were closed for the night. When Lloyd pulled into a garden apartment, I didn't lay back but pulled in right beside her. After she stopped her car, she just sat there and stared at me, her windows up. She said something I couldn't make out, and I motioned for her to roll down a window.

"Why are you following me?" she asked after lowering the passenger-side window halfway.

I opened the door of my jeep. It sat in the shadows of a wall separating the apartments from the street. On the other side of the wall you could hear the occasional car pass by. "I want to talk to you, Rebecca."

"I've told you all I know."

"I don't think so."

"Miss Chase, I don't have any reason to keep secrets from you."

"Except about your relationship with Daryl Flaxx."

She bristled. "There is no relationship."

"Yes—and that's the problem."

Her nose elevated. "I'm certainly not carrying any torch for Daryl."

"Rebecca, help me out here."

"I could call the police."

"You saw them haul me downtown. Know why they let me go?" When she didn't answer, I said, "Because they don't give a damn what happened to Nancy."

"I—I don't see why it's my business either."

"Then I guess you'll walk the picket line until you disappear, too."

"You think Daryl—Mr. Flaxx had something to do with the . . . disappearance?"

"You'll never know unless you answer some questions."

"But I've told you everything I know."

"Rebecca, why don't you let me decide that?"

"I'm supposed to talk to you and be at the Blouse tomorrow if the others don't show up?" She raised the window, then opened her own door, got out, and looked over the top of her car. "I don't think so. I think I'd better get some sleep and you'd best leave."

I got out of my jeep and walked around to her side of the car. "Kathy Gierek moved out of her trailer, but her parents think she's still at the beach. She didn't go home."

Lloyd considered this. "Then it's left to me, isn't it?"

"And somehow I don't think that disappoints you."

"I—I don't know what you're talking about."

"If you can't work at the Open Blouse, you'll walk the picket line. That ought to get Flaxx's attention."

"Miss Chase, I have absolutely no interest in Daryl Flaxx, except to settle the strike. And he will settle. In our favor."

"That doesn't mean he'll take you back."

"He'll have to. It'll be in the settlement."

"It doesn't mean you'll be welcome in his bed."

Up went the freckled nose again. "I don't know where you got this idea I want to sleep with Daryl." She reached inside the car and pulled out her pack. "I didn't sleep with him when I worked there and I won't when the strike's settled."

"Is that why you left?"

"Of course not, you've got this all—"

An apartment door opened and I whirled around, my hand going to my fanny pack.

A sleepy-eyed young man in dark pajamas stuck out his head. "Could you hold this conversation somewhere else? I *may* have to sleep on the couch tonight, but I still need my sleep." And he closed the door very firmly.

Lloyd and I stared at the door, then looked at each other. We couldn't help smiling, then laughing. At least some woman held the upper hand with her man tonight.

"I guess you might as well come on up, Miss Chase."

"Susan."

"Okay. Susan."

Lloyd slung the pack over her shoulder, then gestured toward a breezeway. "But I have to warn you, Cheryl didn't show up and I had to pull her shift. I'm not sure I'll be much use to you."

"I've been up since six and have to do it again tomorrow." I glanced at my watch. "This morning."

"Can't you sleep in?" she whispered, taking the stairs. "I thought private detectives were self-employed."

"I'm looking for Nancy on behalf of Sammy and I don't think he can afford me."

"Nancy can't afford you either," said Lloyd, climbing to the second floor. "She hasn't made any money since Flaxx threw us out." Looking over her shoulder, she added, "And I have no romantic interest in that man, no matter what you might think. I want to make that clear before we start."

Yeah, yeah. Whatever.

The apartments surrounded a courtyard containing several wooden benches under a huge oak tree. The oak's limbs, laden with Spanish moss, reached the second story, some spreading over the roof. Ferns hung in baskets along the portico and beach towels dried on a wrought iron railing. Where the swimming pool was I had no idea.

Color Me Gone

At the third door, Lloyd dropped her shoes outside—I did the same—then fished a key out of her backpack and turned the key in the lock. The furniture was white wicker and also home to a stereo and stacks of CDs. From the kitchen, Lloyd asked if I'd like a beer and I said yes.

She came out of the kitchen with two bottles: Carolina Blonde, a local brew. "If you don't mind, I'd like to get out of this suit. After a couple of shifts, it gets old."

Tell me about it. I was still wearing a one-piece under my rain gear and beginning to chafe. Somewhere along the way I should've taken it off, but with the rain it made more sense to finish the night without having something else to wash—if I ever did. I asked to use Lloyd's facilities and wished I hadn't. A rest room at a truck stop would've been cleaner.

Lloyd came out of the bedroom wearing flip-flops. She turned on the stereo and Jewel began to sing. Besides her flip-flops, she wore a green terry cloth robe open to where I could see the edge of her boobs. The lower end of the robe had fallen open to her thigh, revealing skinny legs, which on my darkest days I sometimes long for.

"Kathy's neighbor said Kathy didn't tell her where she was going."

"That would be Mrs. Tudor. She treated Kathy like her own daughter."

"How long did you know Kathy?"

Lloyd dropped her flip-flops and pulled her feet up under her. "When I came to the Blouse she was already working there. She had the idea for the strike. Carol Andrews got pregnant, and of course Daryl—I mean, Mr. Flaxx—didn't have any insurance. Carol couldn't work, which all of us know is a hazard, having children while you're in your prime. The hospital bills about bankrupted her.

"Kathy went to Flaxx and told him they had to do something about insurance. In South Carolina you aren't required to have health coverage. It's something companies do to be competitive. Flaxx said he didn't care who left and he'd fire the whole bunch of us if we struck. Daryl did, and Harold

94

and a couple of other guys harassed us until Kathy called that lawyer who got Shannon Faulkner into the Citadel. She got the court to define what we could do and what Harold and his buddies couldn't do—to us. After that they pretty much left us alone."

"The court order didn't seem to bother Harold tonight."

"Harold's not very bright, Susan."

And neither are you, my dear. Any attorney worth her billable hours could've had Harold jailed for what he did tonight, but that won't happen while you're enamored with Daryl Flaxx, will it?

"She's preparing a brief which includes a prior judgment in California where health insurance is provided for topless workers."

"Because he charges you to use the facilities."

"You do understand our position, don't you?"

"Actually, I'm more interested in finding Nancy for her son."

"Sammy doesn't care about his mother," she said, following this with another swig of beer. "Everyone knows that."

"Someone has to take an interest. You know how Nancy is."

"And men love that innocence. And those tits. She can really make those tassels fly." Lloyd glanced at her open robe. "Wish I had more myself."

"Larry Joyner's mother said he's at the Braves' games. Could Kathy be with him?"

Lloyd shook her head and pulled her robe close. "Kathy and Larry broke up. But I guess they could've kissed and made up for this particular weekend."

"Why's that?"

"Larry likes his Braves and Kathy was a die-hard Cubs fan. They bought the tickets together—earlier in the year."

"Have you seen Joyner since Kathy disappeared?"

"I saw him in the Blouse last week. That's where they met. Larry didn't approve of the strike and that's why they broke up." She looked at me, puzzled. "But I thought you said they ran off together."

"That's what Mrs. Tudor said. Moved out in the middle of the night. Have there been others, besides Cheryl, who haven't pulled their weight?"

"Some have found other jobs. They know when September comes, the Grand Strand's going to die and they'll need some money."

"What will you do?"

After another swallow of beer, she said, "Keep on keeping on. Kathy's father was a union worker and came down and gave us a pep talk about persisting, even when things looked the darkest. I might have him down before Labor Day—to pump up the girls and let them know what our long-range plan is. But if Kathy's dropped out, I don't know . . . ."

Putting down my beer, I asked, "Tell me, Rebecca, have any other girls disappeared?"

"I don't think anyone's really disappeared. Quit, but not vanished."

"How about those who didn't walk the picket line? Someone who simply left."

"A couple of the girls said they might cross the street and work for the competition, but I guess they went home because I haven't heard of them anywhere along the Strand."

"Could you give me their names and addresses?"

"Why?"

"I'd like to see if any of those girls actually made it home."

12

According to Lloyd, Jennifer Frank was the type of daughter *your* parents always wanted *you* to be: high SAT score, honor roll, and excellent soccer player with college scholarship offers—except that she harbored a deep resentment toward her parents for having to measure up. But Jennifer didn't know that until she went off to the University of North Carolina and crawled out from underneath her parents' thumb.

Besides hitting the books and the ol' soccer ball, Jennifer was expected to keep up her piano lessons and participate in a variety of school activities. Suddenly, at college, she didn't have to answer to anyone. First, her grades went into the toilet and then her scholarship. Soon her parents didn't recognize their daughter: long stringy hair, baggy and unmatched clothing, cigarette smoking—grass when out of their sight. After dropping out of Carolina, the former golden girl drifted to the beach. There she heard about the money to be made dancing topless. Wearing a new click bra from Victoria's Secret, Jennifer was immediately given a tryout at the Open Blouse.

"It's Flaxx's way of weeding out those who can get up in front of a crowd and take off their clothes from those who can't," Lloyd told me. "Lots of girls come in, sometimes in groups, often on a dare. Ones who come in alone he immediately puts up on stage, and if he likes what he sees, he pays them more for one night's work than they've made in a week anywhere else. It's quite an incentive."

"And Jennifer made the cut?"

"Jennifer was wild, and I mean really wild. She had all these rules while growing up. She was ready to cut loose and have a good time. She gave Daryl a hard time the whole time she worked there."

"Sleep with him?"

Lloyd shook her head. "They fought too much and Daryl was always telling her if she didn't like it here, she could always go home to Mom and Dad. That would make Jennifer flip out and she'd quit again. One day she quit for good."

"Never returned?"

"Never."

"Ever see her along the Strand?"

Lloyd shook her head. "Nope."

"Dancing at other topless joints?"

"Never heard of it," she said, downing what was left of her beer. "No—Jennifer didn't take another job. She went home, made up with her family, and went back to school. Otherwise, why haven't we heard from her?"

Agatha Mitchem, called "Aggie" by her friends, ran away from North Georgia, straight across South Carolina, and almost into the ocean. According to Lloyd, Mitchem considered leaping into that ocean. Fortunately, the only bridge high enough to kill you is the one in Charleston, so Aggie was in the wrong place for that type of suicide. She'd have to find another way and she did. Drugs.

A good number of devils chased Aggie out of Georgia. The first was her father, a sheet metal worker who was prone to drink. His wife, pregnant most of the time—there were six kids when Aggie left home—couldn't control him. When she tried, she was likely to receive the back of his hand for her trouble. Molested by her father, Aggie lost her virginity and any positive self-image before reaching puberty. As she grew older, Aggie began staying out late, sleeping around, and binge drinking—until her father decided he wanted a pickup instead of some nuisance kid around.

At sixteen, Aggie was traded to Jack Wise for a truck and locked away in a root cellar after a long day of cleaning and playing house. And in that cellar Aggie had plenty of time to think. Jack Wise said he would kill Aggie if she tried to run away. Jack Wise talked a lot about the revenuer he'd killed and buried in the woods over twenty years before. About butchering hogs, shooting deer, killing this, killing that. How long would it be before Jack Wise killed her?

After one particularly brutal day in Jack's bed and around the house, Aggie resolved to escape. She found a piece of glass, and the following morning was waiting for her "husband." Instead of Wise taking her, she took him, slashing the old man across the face. Aggie was out the door and down the road before old Jack knew what hit him. After he turned his dogs loose on her, Aggie cut across the fields and disappeared into the woods. Then it became a race between the dogs and Aggie's young legs as they raced through the woods and across a creek—which Aggie failed to use to her advantage by not drowning her scent and slogging downstream.

As she ran, she glanced over her shoulder, and not looking where she was going, ran into a tree. It knocked the breath out of her and made her see stars. Looking up from where she lay, Aggie decided she'd hide in the tree. Weighing less than a hundred pounds, she scaled as high as she could (if there's anything they teach a girl in North Georgia, it's how to climb a tree) branches swaying under her weight and Aggie trembling and trying to catch her breath. A moment later, the pack of dogs arrived and began yelping. When dusk came they were still barking their heads off—

with no Jack Wise anywhere in sight.

In the middle of the night, Aggie heard a voice shouting for the damn dogs to shut up. Minutes later, a flashlight came though the woods and a young man walked out of the darkness. A couple of good raps across the snouts and the dogs slunk away. That noise was replaced by the sound of crying.

It took a few minutes to convince Aggie that the man below her wasn't Jack Wise or his agent. It took another half-hour for Aggie, in her weakened state, to make her way down the tree, where she fell into the arms of Arthur Robertson, Jack Wise's next-door neighbor.

Robertson took Aggie home. His wife gave Aggie a bath, fed her, and finally dug the whole story out of her. Later that night, after their children and Aggie had gone to bed, the Robertsons discussed what they should do. They did not know that Aggie was listening.

There was only one thing they could do, said Mrs. Robertson. Turn the girl over to the authorities and turn Jack Wise in to the sheriff. Her husband said they had to live with Jack Wise, but the girl—who was she to them? Mrs. Robertson said she wasn't prepared to spend her life raising children around someone as vile as Jack Wise. Her husband finally relented and they went to bed.

Morning found Aggie gone. She had slipped out a window and followed the dirt road—the young farmer tracked her to the blacktop—where she hitched a ride. And about the time Aggie reached Myrtle Beach, Jack Wise was found lying face down in the creek where he'd died of a massive heart attack. The Robertsons could finally breathe a sigh of relief.

Lloyd stood up and stretched. "Aggie liked to tease men with her dancing." Heading for the kitchen, she looked over her shoulder. "It was the only time I ever saw Aggie smile."

Lloyd returned with more beer. I asked what Aggie's beef had been with Daryl Flaxx.

"Drugs." Lloyd took a pull from her new bottle. "It's one

thing to take a red when you're performing and sick and tired of grinding your ass at a bunch of losers. You know, Susan, the more I learn about men, the harder it is to like them. After a while they're not worth the effort."

"So Aggie was into drugs in a big way?"

"She got into them something serious, and I can't say I blame her. Nothing worked out with any of the guys she dated."

Gee, maybe it had something to do with the way she was raised. "How did Flaxx react?"

"Gave her afternoons."

"Afternoons?"

"After five's the best time to make money. Guys are loosening up or showing off for their buddies. Late at night even better—when they've had more than a few—especially weekends. Daryl says the Blouse has to be open so customers know they can drop by and have a drink. The girls hate afternoons, except Fridays."

"So Aggie was finished."

Lloyd nodded again. "It was really starting to show. Her tits just hung on her. At one time she could turn heads no matter where she went. She was the ultimate sweater girl."

"How did she become attractive enough to work in your . . . line of business?"

"Don't look down on us. If I hadn't gone on strike, I'd be knocking down some serious money."

"I didn't mean—"

"I know what you meant. You don't have the nerve so don't be knocking it. But Aggie, like all girls who come to the beach, ran out of money and begin to whore around. What saved Aggie, because you can't be a whore for too long and make it in our trade—those girls look something awful after giving all those blow jobs—was the pimp who picked her up, cleaned her up, and sold her to the right men. One day her pimp was in an automobile accident, and by the time someone else tried to take over his business, Aggie was already dancing at the Open Blouse."

"For Flaxx."

She nodded, drinking again from her beer. The beer she'd gotten for me rested untouched in my hands.

"Was she living with Flaxx?" I asked.

"Yeah," she said with an unexpected smile. "It really pissed Daryl off when Aggie got into drugs. Oh, he doesn't mind a red now and then to keep you sharp, but the needle"—Lloyd shook her head—"once he sees those marks, you're gone. Says he doesn't need the hassle with the cops. I've known dancers to shoot between their toes to hide it."

"So one day she just disappeared?"

"Uh-huh. Guess she went back to Georgia."

"You're kidding."

"Where else was Aggie to go?"

"That's what I plan on finding out."

13

Since I was supposed to be on duty at eight and it was closer to 4 a.m. than 3 a.m., there was nothing to do but pop a red, then leave word on Marvin's machine that I needed a day off, and head inland. I bought a cup of coffee at Circle K—good until the red kicked in—and tooled down the road listening to "Jagged Little Pill." I was in the state capitol about the same time as the city woke up. Cleaning up in the rest room of a BP, I made myself presentable before going to meet Jennifer Frank's parents. I ditched the shorts and a top I'd pulled on to eliminate more chafing from the bathing suit, and changed to a long skirt and short-sleeved blouse, with accessories. I was slipping into flats when some guy knocked on the door.

"Is there someone in there?"

When I didn't reply, he opened the door with a pass key, then stepped back, startled, nearly stepping on the feet of a heavyset woman behind him.

"Sorry, ma'am, but you can't use the rest room as a dressing room, especially this time of the morning."

"Just get her out of there!" shouted the heavyset woman

as she shifted from one foot to the other.

"Left my husband this morning," I said, grabbing the overnight bag. "That bastard's hit me for the last time."

I pushed my way past him and headed for my jeep while the guy tried to figure who he should have the most sympathy for. Behind him the heavyset woman stepped into the john and slammed the door shut, bolting the lock. The manager followed me to my jeep, where I was locking up my gear in the footlocker welded to the floorboard.

"I'm sorry for your troubles, ma'am, but I'm going to have to ask you to change at the Y next time."

"There won't be any next time," I said, climbing into my jeep. "I'm going to find a job and move out on the SOB."

"Good luck to you." He smiled as I settled into my seat. "And we hope, with your new job, you find time to stop by BP for your gas and anything else you need."

I was about to crank the engine when I had a thought. "Do you know how to find Silver Creek Lane in Riverbend? Is that around here?"

He pointed across a street jammed with early morning commuters. "Take the four-lane toward town until you come to a Kentucky Fried Chicken and turn right. Follow that road about two miles until you come to another BP on the left, and Exxon on the right." He smiled. "Don't stop at the Exxon—unless you're going to change clothes." When I didn't smile, he finished with, "Go through the four-way stop, and at the first road bearing off to the right you'll find Riverbend." He looked at me, puzzled. "But I thought you were looking for a job."

"I am," I said, thinking quickly. "I have a friend whose husband might hire me. And I won't forget to stop at BP for my gas."

The Frank property had a deep lawn and a walkway to a gray saltbox with no shutters. Flowers and bushes were tastefully planted and trimmed to complement the house. To my right, a teenager backed out of a three-car garage in a bright, red Miata convertible.

Stepping down from my jeep, I brushed back my hair and made my way up the sidewalk. The girl in the Miata waved. I waved back. Then I was at the steps where heavy, white rockers lined the porch and ferns sat on matching tables. I rang the doorbell and while it chimed, I watched a minivan stop across the street. Two children wearing bathing suits and carrying towels ran out of a white colonial-style home and climbed inside the minivan. After seeing her charges safely inside, the driver said something and her new arrivals buckled their seat belts. As the woman drove away she smiled and waved.

Hmm. This didn't look so bad.

The door opened and I turned around to face a black woman in a starched maid's outfit. "Yes?" she asked.

"Susan Chase to see Mrs. Frank."

"Is she expecting you?"

"She'll want to see me. It's about her daughter."

The black woman glanced at the driveway. "Her daughter just left."

"This is about Jennifer."

The black woman stiffened. "I'm sorry, but Jennifer Frank doesn't live here any longer." And she tried to close the door in my face.

I put a hand against the door, and with all the volleyballs I'd spiked, I easily held it open. "If you don't mind I'd rather hear that from Mrs. Frank."

The black woman stepped back as I entered the foyer. "Miss, if you don't leave, I'll call the police."

"Do that," I said, "if you can get them to leave their do-nuts at this time of day."

In the foyer, an Oriental runner crossed the hardwood floor. A chair and table stood at the base of a stairwell where the runner continued upstairs and made two short turns around a black railing with white balusters. The living room was to my right.

"Tell Mrs. Frank I'll be in here."

"Miss, I don't think—"

Color Me Gone

"And I could use a cup of coffee. Black."

The maid followed me into the room and scanned the place as if memorizing the position of each and every piece of furniture and bric-a-brac. That done, she walked over and closed the French doors between this room and the dining room. Glancing through those doors, I spotted a silver tea service I might like to own. Maybe this woman knew me better than I knew myself.

The living room held overstuffed furniture and a coffee table with an elaborate metal base. Assorted ornate silver bowls sat on its glass top. Beside each chair, an off-white sculptured marble piece served as an end table. Each piece blended in with the stones of a fireplace in which a fire was laid against the first chill. Bookcases recessed into the wall were filled with popular titles, including several books on raising children. A rug ran diagonally across the room and shared a pattern with curtains pulled back to allow the sunlight in. Under one window, and on a matching piece of stone, sat a bonsai tree.

Over the mantle hung a family portrait, but the picture was out of whack. The daughter I'd seen leaving in the Miata sat on a bench beside her mother; on the other side of the mother sat a younger brother. Behind them stood a distinguished-looking father with graying hair and ramrod posture. He was the one who made the picture out of balance—because daughter Jennifer, originally to his right, had been painted out of the portrait!

"Yes?" said a voice behind me.

Standing in the doorway was the woman in the portrait. Healthy tan, blond hair, square head, blue eyes, elegant posture. Mrs. Frank wore a short-sleeved blouse with chocolate brown slacks and leather flats. A simple gold chain hung around her neck, the type that might hold an oval locket for a photograph. An oval locket that could be clutched. And Mrs. Frank was clutching that oval locket when she stepped into the room. "You have news of Jennifer?"

"I thought you might be interested," I said, returning my

gaze to the portrait, "but I see I've come to the wrong house."

The woman glanced at the portrait. "My—my husband had that done. I objected, but Jennifer had hurt him so. Just who are you, Miss Chase?"

"A lifeguard from Myrtle Beach."

"I don't understand. Do you know the whereabouts of my daughter?"

"Perhaps." I gestured at the sofa. "Why don't we have a seat and talk about it?"

"Yes, yes, have a seat, Miss Chase." She nodded as she came around the sofa, which faced the fireplace. "I seem to have misplaced my manners. It's been so long since we've heard anything . . . . Would you like a cup of coffee?"

"I've already asked for one."

She nodded again, then joined me on the sofa. The portrait looked down on us.

Inclining my head in its direction, I asked, "Why not have it taken down? I threw out my mother's."

"What . . . what do you mean?"

"I didn't want to be reminded of her of walking out on the family."

"I—I couldn't do that. What would the other children think?"

"Do you mean 'what would the neighbors think?'" I could hear my voice becoming shrill. Gesturing at the mantle, I added, "What do you think they think when they see this monstrosity on the wall—that your husband is in control?"

More than one parent had employed me to locate his kid, and after finding them, many times I learned it might be best if the runaway never returned home. Grandparents. That was the answer. It might not please Granny, but it sure made me feel righteous.

Mrs. Frank glanced at the floor. She cleared her throat. "This is . . . this is the first time anyone's contacted us in . . . years. We assumed Jennifer was dead. Is she?" The woman held her breath. She gripped the oval locket.

"I have no idea, but I will tell you what I've learned." I

crossed my legs and told her about Jennifer dancing at the Open Blouse.

"We know about that. I wired Jenny money until she got a job at the Open Blouse. You were one of the dancers?"

"Not hardly. I have a friend who performed there and she's disappeared. Her son asked me to find her, but while I was looking into her disappearance, I learned she wasn't the only girl missing. There's a Kathy Gierek, and Agatha Mitchem, and your daughter."

"Those names mean nothing to me."

"Each of these young women performed at the Open Blouse, had a disagreement with management, and disappeared. When I leave here, I'm on my way to track down the family of the last girl." Slowing down to catch my breath, I said, "However, I really doubt she ever returned home. She was abused as a child and swapped for a pickup truck."

Frank's hand fell away from the oval. "Swapped for a pickup . . . truck?"

"Yes," I said, glancing at the portrait. "So your family's not all that odd."

Frank glanced at the painting and clutched the locket again. Jennifer's picture had to be inside that locket.

The maid returned with my coffee and set it on the table. She shot a protective look at Frank, then glared at me before leaving the room. I sipped the coffee. Frank watched me.

"My husband said it would be best to get on with our lives . . . since Jennifer had turned her back on us."

"Has it worked?" I asked, putting down the cup. The coffee was pretty good, actually.

"Not for me. I want to know everything you've learned about Jennifer."

"I wish I could tell you more. I was hoping you could tell me something . . . Now that I find she's not here, I really don't know what to think but the worst."

The woman clutched the oval and began to cry softly.

Damn you, Chase, when are you going to learn people can't take your candor?

Steve Brown

Hey, I'm not the one who married such a jerk.

Mrs. Frank wiped the tears away. "I'll—I'll pay for you to find her. Anything you ask."

"I already have a client." Yeah, right, and how much has Peanut paid for your services?

"But you'd be looking for my daughter at the same time."

"I'll be glad to let you know what I learn. When was the last time you saw Jennifer?"

"It was . . . ."

The woman couldn't hold back the tears, and as if on cue the maid returned with a box of Kleenex. The maid left the box on the corner of the table and the look she gave me told me she still might call the police.

After drying her tears, Mrs. Frank said, "It was almost two years ago. She was doing that horrid dancing. I didn't know what to tell my friends. Edmund tells people Jennifer is no longer part of this family." She gestured at the portrait. "Edmund worked hard to have the things we have. His father came over from the Netherlands when he was just a boy. Jennifer is actually first generation American—on his side. I met him at Carolina when he came there to study international business. And Edmund *has* been a success, working his way up and now running the company."

She looked into her lap again. "All Edmund wanted was the best for our children. I'm—I'm not saying Edmund doesn't have his faults, but he gave Jennifer every opportunity and she threw those opportunities away. It was horrible . . . the fights they had . . . . When Edmund and I were first married, he took a job in Washington working for the Commerce Department. Edmund said it would give him an overview of companies when he switched to the private sector. Edmund planned every step of his career and he couldn't understand why our daughter wouldn't do the same."

"It really depends on what your kid wants."

Mrs. Frank straightened up. "What would an eighteen-year-old girl know about life, Miss Chase, about once-in-a-lifetime opportunities such as a full scholarship to the University of North Carolina?"

"You're preaching to the wrong person." I put down my coffee. "I've been on my own since I was fifteen. I don't know about any opportunities except the ones I make myself."

"And what have you done with those opportunities?"

"Survived."

Agatha Mitchem's family was a bit harder to find. They'd moved several times, in the area around Rome, Georgia. The Chamber of Commerce was most helpful—when I told them Norman Mitchem owed me some money. They said for me to get in line, that the Top Notch Credit Bureau was handling any collections it could squeeze out of Norman Mitchem.

At Top Notch Credit, I flashed my ID and was given the last known address. I could tell there was no love lost between Top Notch and Norman Mitchem . . . who lived in a run-down section of town, all white and all poor. I parked against a broken curb and crossed a weed-filled yard to a set of dilapidated steps. Carefully climbing to the porch I knocked on the door. Arriving in Rome, I had gone to another service station and changed into another blouse. Now I wished I hadn't. Any class act would be totally lost on these people. The thermometer stood at ninety, and once my jeep comes to a stop, that's when the air-conditioning stops.

Mrs. Mitchem peered through the screen door. She had brown hair in her face, wore a faded dress and no makeup. She possessed a stocky, serviceable body built for having babies—lots of babies, it would appear. On her hip was a child of indeterminate age and sex and clinging to the hem of her frayed dress was another baby wearing only a diaper. If they were lucky, these kids were all boys.

"Whatever you're selling, we ain't interested."

"I'm looking for your daughter—Aggie."

The woman stepped back, taking the baby with her. The one attached to her hem was taken by surprise and didn't move quickly enough. It was pulled backwards and plopped to the floor on its diapered bottom where it started squawking.

"Why would you be asking me 'bout her? Aggie don't live here no more."

"Yes, yes, I know. Your husband swapped her for a pickup truck." Nothing like the direct approach. Hit them between the eyes and see what falls out—of their mouth.

"I don't know nothing about that. That was between Aggie and my husband."

"Swapping her for a pickup—she had a say in that?" All but forgotten was the child wailing at the woman's feet.

"Aggie was always saying she wanted to get married and move out, so my husband married her off to Jack Wise, and Jack—he gave my husband a truck. And there weren't nothing illegal 'bout it. Daddies around the world fix up their daughters with husbands and get something in return. A dowry it's called. We seen it on the Discovery Channel."

"First I've heard of it occurring here."

"That's where you're wrong. It's been done before. I was fixed up with my husband."

They didn't do you any favors, did they? "What do you hear from Aggie?"

"Why nothing."

"Because Jack locked her in his root cellar every night?"

Mitchem glanced past me to my jeep. "I don't think I'd best be talking to you. My husband warned me folks wouldn't understand. Aggie has a good chance to inherit all Jack's property when he dies."

"Not unless she has a marriage license."

"Listen, lady, you better git out of here, whoever you are. I don't have to talk to you. I don't have to talk to anyone. My husband told me that. You come back and talk with him, if'n you got any questions."

"Never happen. Just dropped by to find out what county Jack Wise lives in."

"Why it's Dilbert. Why didn't you say so in the first place? Take the state highway north 'til you come to Edwards Corners. Anyone there can tell you how to find Jack's place." When I turned to go, she added, "And tell Aggie I said, 'hi.'"

Color Me Gone

At Edwards Corners I was given directions by an old coot at a general store: Follow the two-lane seven and eight-tenths miles to an old Gulf station that went out of business when the interstate came through. Then fourteen and three-tenths miles on county road 290 to where there's a shelter for kids waiting to catch the school bus.

At the shelter, which had weeds growing out of it, I turned up a narrow, rutted road winding into the hills a mile and a half. It took almost twenty minutes to cover this last bit. The rutted road split ten minutes into the drive, the road on the left to Jack Wise's former property, the one on the right to the Arthur Robertsons'. Not being all that interested in visiting root cellars, I continued to the right, and ten minutes later came over the last hill and rode down into a small valley.

The valley was planted with corn, and against the rear wall stood the house. Riding through the fields, I could make out tomatoes, squash, and string beans, which if properly preserved would make a family fairly self-sufficient. Other items were planted among the corn, which ensured the Robertsons' self-sufficiency.

In the far corner of the valley, a man rode a tractor. I don't know if he saw me, but his kids certainly did, clamoring out of the house when I pulled to a stop. A mismatched group of dogs on the porch raised their heads and examined me as the children surrounded my jeep. There were three of them, all girls, and all wore clean dresses like kids attending a Christian school: plenty of flowers, not enough color, and too many ruffles.

A woman carrying a bowl walked onto the porch of a house that looked like it had been built by hand and been there forever: clapboard sides and chimney in the center. I saw no hint of electricity, no fans in the windows or satellite dish, but there were plenty of open windows. I could see a well to one side of the path leading to a barn. In the corral a horse swung his tail at flies. In a sty, pigs slept and snorted in the mud. Uphill, where there wasn't much chance of planting anything, cows drank at a trough. Climbing down from my jeep, I noticed the temperature had dropped considerably since I'd left Edwards Corners. The woman stood higher than I did as the house's foundation was made of stone and probably harbored a cellar. I shivered in the late afternoon sun.

Mrs. Robertson was middle-aged, as round as she was tall, and wore a dress of the same type as her girls. The garment was protected by an apron splattered with flour and eggs. She continued to stir the bowl cradled in her arm as she looked me over. Her hair was brown and chopped off, her arms and face were brown. She looked like a round, brown pixie.

She asked if I was lost.

"Not if you're Mrs. Robertson." I put a foot on the stairs leading to the porch.

The hand stopped its stirring. "You're not with the school district, are you? I'm doing just fine teaching the girls at home. We won't be needing the county's help this fall."

I glanced at my blouse and skirt. Seems some folks can be impressed—if they're paranoid about what they're farming. "You've had trouble with them before?"

"They want the children to go to school in town and I want to teach them at home. They said if we didn't let them go, they'd take them away from us."

"Doesn't seem right," I said, playing along, "folks being told what to do about raising their own kids." What was up with this? Home schooling was all the rage.

"That's what Arthur and I told them, but they said we weren't qualified to teach what they needed to fit into the modern world." She harrumphed, then spit a shot of brown chewing tobacco in the dirt beside me. One of the dogs raised his head to see where the stream hit. Satisfied, the animal put his head back down and stared at me with mournful eyes. "If I wanted them to be part of the modern world I wouldn't be living out here." She gestured at the farm. "What can I do for you, Miss?"

"Chase, Susan Chase."

She squinted. "You're not from around here, are you?"

"No, ma'am, I'm not."

"And you work outside. I can tell by the tan." She glanced at her own arms. "Heard the modern world doesn't like them kind of tans anymore. Gives them cancer or some such nonsense. Nowadays people believe anything the government tells them." She snorted, then spit into the dirt again. The dog raised his head and checked her accuracy. Well, there wasn't a lot of excitement around these parts.

"I'm a lifeguard at Myrtle Beach."

"Myrtle Beach?" asked the woman, raising her eyebrows. "You're a long way from home."

"I'm looking for a friend of a friend. I was hoping you could help me find her."

"And who would this friend of your friend be?"

"Aggie Mitchem."

"Don't know her," she said too quickly.

"Someone at Myrtle Beach said this girl stayed a night with you two years ago."

To the children, she said, "Into the house, girls."

Now the whining began. What did you expect? I might be the only person from the "modern world" they'd seen lately.

After the kids had disappeared inside, the woman put her bowl on the ledge of one of the open windows and came over to the steps. The dog raised his head, looked at the bowl, then at the round little woman, and put down his head. Children's faces appeared at the window.

The woman lowered her voice. "Miss Chase, we don't want any trouble."

"I simply want to know if Aggie returned here when she left the Grand Strand several months ago."

"Now why would she do a thing like that?"

"Mrs. Robertson, my friend says Aggie broke down that night your husband rescued her and told you about being swapped for a pickup, about being locked in a root cellar, and how she slashed Jack Wise's face with a piece of glass."

"You seem to know quite a bit."

"I'm telling you this so I can go away and leave you alone. I have no interest in you or your family"—I scanned the valley of green—"or what you're doing here."

"What we're doing here? What you mean 'what we're doing here?' We're minding our own business."

"And planting marijuana among your corn."

She eyed me. "You sure you ain't with the government?"

I opened my purse and held up my ID. "I'm private." Putting the ID away, I added, "I'm not going to tell the government what you're doing because they'd come out here, find you growing grass, and put you in jail and your kids in foster homes. I've lived in a foster home, Mrs. Robertson. I wouldn't wish that on anyone." I glanced at the window where the faces stared at us. "I certainly wouldn't wish it on your babies."

"I could lie to you and you'd never know it."

Looking where the tractor was being worked, I said, "You know, Mrs. Robertson, it's about impossible to make a living with such a small farm unless you have something on the side. They used to make whiskey up in these hills, but there's no money in that these days, not with the profits to be made in grass. What other work does your husband do, other than that which involves late night visits to Atlanta and selling his load? The government doesn't need me to figure this out, and the highest priority is given to calls made by private citizens. You know, the kind who vote for congressmen who approve budgets for government agencies."

Robertson gazed over the valley for a minute or two. "Aggie come back to see us after she moved to the beach. Told us she had a job and didn't ever have to go home. But said she owed it to us to come back and tell us she was doing okay after what Arthur done for her. After that all we got was cards and letters."

I said nothing. It was her party.

"Listen, I don't know who you are, young lady, and who you really work for, but that girl was messed up. That's the reason why Arthur and I moved out here. If the city could do it to Aggie, it could do it to one of our own." She glanced at the window with her children's faces peering out. "You kids find something to do."

They whined, but not for long. The hound raised his head, looked at the window, then put his head down.

"We had only been out here little more than a year, and I was having second thoughts about what we'd done with our lives—our children's, too—when the good Lord sent Aggie into our lives."

"Pardon?" Sometimes I don't understand people's interpretation of the scriptures.

"To let us know it was right to turn our back on the city and its wickedness. When Arthur inherited this place, we packed it in with the world." She glanced toward the window. "That way our girls will always know they have a safe place to come home to if'n what they do outside this valley don't work out."

"And that's why Aggie returned, isn't it?"

"I just told you she didn't come but that one time."

"Sorry, Mrs. Robertson, but your family stood out among all the wretchedness that had been her life so far. You did something no other person ever did. You cared. So Aggie had to return. And I'm guessing she did that on more than one occasion."

The woman stared at me for the longest, then said, "Up until several months ago Aggie visited us twice a year, but always returned to that wickedness at Myrtle Beach. And I think it was like you said: She wanted to have a place to call home. Aggie used to drive in here in her fancy car and wearing her flashy clothing. I spoke to her about that. The girls were getting the wrong idea. They've been taught how people sell their souls for a few pretties. After that, Aggie wore dresses whenever she'd come home, ones like my girls and myself wear. You're right, Miss Chase. No matter what people might think of us, Aggie Mitchem considered this place home."

14

"So what do you think you have, Susan?"
I was in the galley of Dads' schooner. He was fixing dinner while I was trying to decide between Tony Bennett and Frank Sinatra. Dads has all their CDs, remastered and sounding surprisingly better than some of the music I generally dance to. Then again, you can't snuggle into a guy dancing to hip-hop.

I'd returned from Georgia last night. After sleeping all day, I was trying to sort out what I knew from what I could only speculate about. That's why I was with Dads, not merely for supper. Unknown to me, Dads had another agenda.

Peanut sat on a stool, dressed like a little man again and watching the two of us. His dark eyes shifted from one to the other.

"What do I *think* I've got? I *know* what I've got." I'd go with Tony. Sometimes, the way Bennett sang made me tingle all over, especially when I was dancing with Chad. Like that would ever happen again.

Dads turned away from the stove, stainless steel pot in one hand, plastic spoon in the other. It appeared I was going to eat vegetables for a change.

Dads real name is Harry Poinsett. He's a descendant of the fellow who christened the scarlet-leafed plant you decorate your house with at Christmas. I prefer to call him "Dads." Dads says it implies intimacy without being close. Harry says stuff like that. He's a retired diplomat. Dads was in Turkey when our ambassador was car-bombed. He said that after being held hostage by the Iranians, "third time's the charm," and he happily took early retirement. His wife was not pleased with life in the slow lane. She lives in Columbia, South Carolina, and runs with the university crowd.

A balding fellow in his early sixties, with a graying beard, Dads knows the school system gave short shrift to my generation. Us Twentysomes were expected to learn the New Math in open classrooms, fill in the blanks when it came to sex and drugs, and never think about how fortunate we were to have survived The Pill.

This evening, Harry wore an off-white pullover with a pair of navy blue slacks and running shoes. Thin almost to the point of emaciation, Dads doesn't eat much. I suspect that's because he might balloon in weight. Photographs on the bulkhead show a different Harry Poinsett, the diplomat, complete with spare tire.

"Run it by me again, Susan, because I have to say I tend to agree with Lieutenant Warden."

With this, Peanut slipped out of his chair and disappeared topside. Poor kid. Still searching for the perfect family. Well, we all have our crosses to bear.

"Don't go too far, Samuel. Dinner is about ready."

How does Harry make us be on time? Last time I got in a huff and walked out, it was almost a week before we spoke and over a month before I was invited to another meal. A tough feat when you're moored next-door. Harry must've seen my disdain for Peanut as he went up the stairs. All the work I'd done for the little twit and not one word of thanks.

"Young Samuel is understandably concerned about his mother, Susan."

Steve Brown

"We all have mothers we're concerned about."

Dads shook his head and returned to his vegetables. A whole chicken broiled inside the oven, later to be accompanied by rice. All in all, between Dads and Mrs. Tudor, my quota of decent meals should be filled for the next month.

"Then run it by me, just as you did Lieutenant Warden."

I snorted. "Warden's got more important things to do than look for some topless dancers."

"Well, you can understand his position."

"Yes—it's identical to the one held by the Chamber of Commerce."

Harry glanced at me. "Don't you think that's a little harsh?"

"You men have a problem with women and pedestals. We're not as sweet as you think."

"But we don't want to know about that."

"Warden looks down his nose at Nancy Noel and the other girls. Personally, I wouldn't care to get up in front of a bunch of horny guys and take off my clothes, but I don't look down on others for doing it. They've just figured an angle people like me can only be jealous of."

Dads sighed as he stirred the different pots, moving from one to the other, a different spoon for each dish. "Against a foe I can defend myself, but heaven protect me from a blundering friend." He went on to add, "I'd like to help, Princess, but you disappeared on me again."

I leaned against the bulkhead. It would be a long time before I remembered that I'd never put on Sinatra or Bennett, and by that time I would be miles away from the Landing. "I've been busy tracking four young women who disappeared from the Open Blouse after having run-ins with the management. Two of them supposedly left town with boyfriends, but I can find no evidence either girl had a boyfriend. One of the boyfriends was seen at the Open Blouse with a bunch of his cronies the week after his girlfriend disappeared. He's in Atlanta at a ball game and I haven't been able to talk with him. Or determine if Kathy Gierek's with him. The other girl, who was on strike, wasn't known to have a steady boyfriend"—I glanced at

119

the hatch leading topside—"but a series of one-night stands."

"Samuel's mother," Dads said, after closing the oven door and standing up.

"Yes—all four were strippers between the ages of twenty and thirty-five. And blond."

"Susan, I would think just about every girl who works in such an establishment would be a blonde, in some fashion or another. Just part of the job description, like having an ample chest."

"The one walking the picket line was a redhead and not particularly well-endowed."

"That would add to the mix."

"Mix?" I came off the bulkhead. "Sweet Jesus, Harry, don't tell me you approve of this. It's only one step removed from the Miss America Pageant." I told him about the woman dressed as a business executive, stripping to the jeers and catcalls of men until she was in tears, her clothes ripped and torn from her body.

"And who ripped those clothes off? She did it as part of the show. Really, you have to get over your hostility toward such male foolishness. Men simply have different interests."

"One particular one, and we know what that is."

"You've certainly used it to your advantage, as have many young women."

"I don't want to be a piece of meat to any man."

"Then what are you doing when you fix your hair and dress up?"

"I hardly ever fix my hair."

"Well, then, what about that bathing suit you wear?"

"It comes with the job."

"So did the girl's business suit—the one pretending to allow those men to reduce her influence and power."

I shivered, wrapping my arms around myself. There was something wrong here and I didn't understand what it was. "May I have a drink?"

"You know where the bar is," he said without looking up from the stove.

Moving into the next cabin, I mixed very little water with some very good bourbon, then shivered again. Women were being used and violated, and Dads was telling me to cool it, that it had always been this way.

Perhaps that was what was bothering me. Things would never change—not when there were women who were willing to dress up and act out such fantasies. And this was not only okay in sleazy strip clubs, but encouraged in suburbia by Victoria's Secret.

I sipped my bourbon and wondered how much my feelings were in direct proportion to my having lost Chad Rivers. Maybe, in my heart of hearts, I wished I was taking off my clothes for him.

Correction! With him!

To hell with this! I was getting carried away over some guy, and I'd never before allowed myself such an indulgence.

I finished my drink, then fixed another and returned to the galley. Taking a seat on one of the stools, I said, "So it stands to reason if I had a job at the Open Blouse, if I could actually stand to work there, and got into a fight with Daryl Flaxx, I would also disappear. Without a trace. Because I'm blond."

"It's a little late to go undercover, Princess."

But what was it time for? I wasn't going to call Chad. I wouldn't give him the satisfaction. My shoulders slumped as I stared into my glass.

"You actually think Daryl Flaxx has girls bashed over the head, then taken out and dropped into some sinkhole in the state park?"

I looked up. "The thought had crossed my mind."

"And you told this to Lieutenant Warden?"

"I told his voice mail. Warden wasn't in when I called. He's never in when I call. I think he uses the fucking voice mail to screen his calls."

"Please watch you language. Remember, you promised. What time did you leave the message?"

"You don't want to know."

He shook his head and slid some brown-and-serve rolls into the oven. "Driving across Carolina in the middle of the night, and without a good night's sleep, that has to concern someone. If not you, then me."

"I did okay, Dads."

"Ah, yes, young people. Never get sick, never die, and never grow old."

"This conversation's getting old."

"What do you expect Lieutenant Warden to do?"

"He *has* done something. While I was in Georgia, Warden stopped by and talked to Flaxx. I had a letter when I got back, from Warden, notifying me to back off, that he had found no connection between the missing girls and the Open Blouse. Girls leave there all the time."

"That's all it said?"

I took a quick drink from my glass. "He included a copy of a log of the conversations Flaxx had with the women who were fired or left over some disagreement. An exit log Flaxx uses to cover his ass. He must have a recording device in his office."

"So he can't be brought up on sexual harassment charges."

"Bring a sexual harassment suit in that place? That'd be the last place a woman would have a case." After another sip of my drink, I asked, "What'd you learn?"

"So Lieutenant Warden investigated, found nothing of substance, and passed along the information to you. That was considerate of him."

"Let's stick to Daryl Flaxx."

"Before we do, how about Chad Rivers?"

"Daryl Flaxx, Dads. Please."

Harry chuckled. "Love doesn't make the world go around, Susan. It's what makes the ride worthwhile." He saw the look on my face and changed his tone. "Not much to report, my dear. Daryl Flaxx is from New Jersey and didn't do that well in high school, but he's very bright, has a high IQ."

"High school probably didn't challenge him. That's why I dropped out."

"Uh-huh, and I always thought you were a discipline problem."

"How did you learn about Flaxx's IQ?"

"I still have friends in high places, the army to mention one."

"Flax was in the service?"

Dads nodded. "When he was a teenager he hung around the mob, running numbers, doing a little body work. The last time he got into trouble—when he was nineteen—the judge gave him a choice of joining the army or going to prison. He was later discharged for selling liquor from the officers' club off base. He was part of a scheme to smuggle liquor into Saudi Arabia during Operation Desert Storm."

"I'll bet the army loved that. I met a guy from Sumter Air Force Base who told me they had these ships at sea during the Gulf Wars so you could have a beer. They'd bring in girls to sing and strip and put on a show. Something that didn't appear on CNN."

"Susan, the young people fighting in Iraq didn't stop being human just because they were moved to another part of the world. There were several pregnancies, engagements, and—"

"Rapes!" I said, spilling bourbon all over my hand.

"Yes, rapes occurred while our troops were overseas. At least one soldier was brought up on murder charges. Anyway, the army gave Flaxx a dishonorable discharge, and when they did, Flaxx remembered all those strip joints he'd been to as an enlisted man and how liquor flowed like wine, though I don't think that's quite the proper simile."

"But he couldn't go home because of the mob."

"He would've had to pay for protection. Anyway, most people from New Jersey have been to Myrtle Beach, so Flaxx came down here and brought along a couple of girls who were later picked up for turning tricks in the parking lot of his first nightclub."

"So don't you see what I'm getting at here?"

He looked at me from the stove. "Yes, but I don't think

Flaxx is making them disappear. There's nothing in his past that points to that."

"What about the body work he did for the mob?"

"Princess, please. Beating up people who are slow pays is quite different from knocking young women over the head and dumping them in sinkholes. Anyway, Flaxx opened the Open Blouse like any other topless place, then realized if there were all these 900 phone numbers turning men on with their fantasies, that he needed to put on more of a show. It's the wave of the future, Susan, delivering more for your entertainment buck. Flaxx is in competition with anyone who wants that entertainment dollar along the Grand Strand."

"You're starting to even sound like him. For the record, I think some of the acts he puts on stage are sick and perverted."

"We've already covered that, Princess. Perhaps you should stick to locating runaways, then you'll know who the bad guys are: the parents." He returned to the stove. "So what's your status with Chad Rivers?"

"There was a message on my machine for me to call him."

"And have you?" he asked, looking at me.

"I've been busy catching up on my sleep."

"I think you should call him."

"I probably will."

"Why do you hesitate?"

Staring at the floor, I said, "He acts like he's hot stuff."

"Chad Rivers isn't the only one who thinks they're 'hot stuff.'"

I slid off the stool. "My God, Harry! Some good-looking moneybags comes along and you people fall all over yourselves trying to get me married. This is so frigging bogus!"

"Let's just say I don't find many articles in the women's magazines touting the virtues of letting all the good ones get away."

"As your wife did with you?"

"Switching to my problems won't solve your problem."

"Problem? What problem is that?"

"If you're not going back to school or finding another career path, what are you planning to do with the rest of your life? Lifeguarding doesn't become you."

"The independence does."

"Maybe when you were a teenager, but that's in the past."

"I'm still young."

"But with fewer prospects."

"Dads, I had no idea you felt this way."

"My dear," he said, stirring one of his pots, "I'm only pointing out that young men like Chad Rivers don't come along every day, nor do they often show interest in young women working dead-end jobs."

My hands went to my hips, "I think I've had enough of this conversation."

"Susan, please don't be unpleasant. It was purely an academic discussion"—he smiled—"like the one we were having about topless dancing."

"It damn well wasn't, and I damn well know where you got your information about Flaxx. You've been talking with Warden behind my back."

"My dear, we have only your best interests at heart."

"What bull! You only want to control me." And I went up the ladder and got the hell out of there.

"Don't go far," he called after me. "Dinner's almost ready."

"Yes," I shouted, after noticing Sammy Noel on the bow of the schooner, "it's ready for someone who'll fall in line with what you think he should do with his life."

That's the last thing I remember before waking up in a small, windowless room. Well, not exactly. I do remember changing my mind about going home to drink myself into a complete stupor. Uh-huh. Next time I'll listen to my conscience.

Instead I scuffled down the road, trying to work off my anger at Dads wanting me to get married and the fact that I didn't have a clue about finding Nancy or any of the other women. That was soon taken out of my hands.

I was muttering to myself and kicking up pieces of the shell road when I noticed a car parked beside the pines with its hood up. In the darkness I saw a burly-shaped man bent over the engine of a four-door sedan.

"Got a problem?" I asked, strolling over. I'm fairly handy when it comes to engines.

In the light from the flashlight, I could see he had thick shoulders, solid arms, and a barrel chest. He was dressed in black and his face was dark, not Negroid but something else. I knew that face from somewhere . . . . His long-sleeved shirt was rolled up to the elbows and there was plenty of hair on his arms.

"The engine . . . it started sputtering," he said with an accent, like from England.

"Who are you looking for?" I glanced at the pines that hid me from the Landing. Out of the corner of my eye I saw something come swinging in my direction.

"You—Miss Chase!"

15

The next thing I knew, I was lying on a narrow bed in a small, dimly lit, windowless room, a knot on the back of my head. I sat up and swung my legs over the side, thought about standing up, but felt better sitting down. The frigging room was moving and the pain in my head was excruciating. One of my arms was sore as if I might've fallen, but there was no bruise, only a small bump.

I'd been given a shot.

A shot of what? How long had I been out? And where the hell was I? Touching the bump on the back of my head brought tears to my eyes. I wiped them away with the back of my hand. I was wearing jeans, a short-sleeved blouse, and running shoes. But my fanny pack and my pistol were gone, as were the contents of my pockets. I looked up at the ceiling. I wouldn't be climbing out of this place.

Uh-huh. By mucking around in the affairs of the Open Blouse, I'd finally graduated to the Big Time, and something I might not be able to talk or climb out of.

When I was finally able to stand, I tottered around the dimly lit room like an old woman. I ran my hands along the walls looking for a door, and found it by feeling a piece of glass affixed to a hole covered with something like chicken wire. I could find no button, knob, or bell, so I slammed my fist on the door.

"Okay, okay, I'm up. What's for breakfast?"

No answer.

I heard a soft, whining noise that came from overhead. I looked up to see a camera taking my measure. Waving at the little machine made me nauseous. I had to lean into the wall to keep from tossing my cookies.

Soon the panel in the door slid back and a woman's face appeared at the tiny window. "Ah, Miss Chase. You are awake."

"Obviously."

The door opened.

"If you will follow me," said the woman in British-accented English. Her face was veiled and her body completely covered with something out of the *Arabian Nights.* What the hell did this have to do with the frigging Open Blouse?

"We had no idea when you would arrive."

"Or where I'd be." All I could see was a pair of dark eyes through the sheer material of the veil. The thing must play havoc with a girl's 'do. "I take it we're not in Kansas anymore."

I could only imagine a smile behind the veil, but I always think I'm much funnier than I actually am. The woman gestured down a hallway that led to a light so bright I had to shade my eyes. Running my hand along the wall to steady myself, I stumbled into a second-story room with modern furniture and glass walls overlooking a courtyard with a small, circular pool. Palm trees were planted in pairs against a high, reddish stone wall. I gulped. Beyond the wall were miles and miles of sand. And where the light brown of the desert met the horizon, the sky was solid, cloudless blue. I made my way into the glass corner and looked left and right, but all I could see was more sand.

Turning around, I scrutinized the room. It contained the

aforementioned modern furniture, over-stuffed chairs and a sofa, a black plastic coffee table with matching end tables, slender floor lamps next to the chairs, and sculptures displayed on shelves built into the wall. Indirect lighting gave the room what little light it needed in corners. The carpet was white and thick enough to cover my running shoes. Not a single plant or flower decorated the room. Instinctively I knew this was a man's room. Or arranged to suit one.

"We simply didn't know when to expect you," prattled on the woman. "First it was two days ago, then yesterday, and last night you were finally here."

"Did I cross through the Stargate?"

The woman stood on the other side of a serving window in a kitchenette. She leaned down to where I could see her veiled face. "Mr. Faisal will be with you shortly and he can answer all your questions." She straightened up so I could see only the black body covering. "What might I prepare for you, Miss Chase, a western style breakfast, perhaps steak and eggs? After the effects of the drug wear off, most of our visitors are terribly hungry."

"I'm terribly hungry to know where I am."

She leaned down again so I could see her veiled face. "Miss Chase, I can understand your concern, but I am only here to address your personal needs. Sometimes there is a reaction to the IV—if you don't have something on your stomach—"

"One of my personal needs is to know where the hell I am." I crossed to the serving window and its barstools. As I did, I examined my arm and found the vein that had been used.

"Perhaps you would like an Alka-Seltzer or a hot bath." She gestured to a door to my left. "In there is a shower and clean clothes."

And another door next to it.

The lady picks Door Number Two.

"You have certainly had a long trip," said the woman.

"To where?" I asked, moving toward the wrong door.

Color Me Gone

The woman came out of the kitchenette with hands be-hind her back. "Mr. Faisal asked that I be put at your disposal, but if you would prefer to return to your room, you can do that just as well."

I reached for the door. "Who's going to make me?"

She whipped out what looked like a can of mace, and before I could leap for her, she sprayed my face. I remember reaching for her. I don't recall hitting the floor.

I woke up on the narrow bed in the windowless room again. One side of my face was sore and puffy, and I had a horrible headache. Still, I hammered on the door, and in a moment the veiled face appeared as the panel slid back.

"Steak and eggs," I said, "Well done and lots of coffee. Black, like your outfit."

"Perhaps a little Coca-Cola to settle the stomach first?" she asked, then opened the door.

"Whatever."

Again I ran my hand across the wall as I followed her down the hallway and into the brightly lit room. I hadn't been dreaming. I was in the middle of the frigging desert—which desert, I had no clue. The Middle East and the top of Africa both have decent deserts. I'd seen them on the Dis-covery Channel. The American Southwest was out of the question because of the woman's costume—unless some-one was trying to trick me. But why would they be doing that?

They're not, Susan. You aren't the center of these people's universe so you'd better start watching your tongue.

The woman turned on the gas stove. "You'll find every-thing you need in the bathroom." And she watched me stagger over to the wrong door again, the one I'd thought about es-caping through on my earlier visit to this room.

No go. Locked up tight. Turning around, I found the woman in the doorway of the kitchenette again, the can of knockout potion in her hand.

I raised my hands in surrender. "Took a wrong turn." I

130

flashed a smile. "It happens."

"Mr. Faisal said you were quite clever, Miss Chase, as I am now learning." She pointed at the correct door.

I used the toilet, and sitting on the john, I looked around. Again no decorations or potpourri. As I went about my business I noticed my hands were shaking—enough to make me dizzy. I dropped to my knees and threw up in the toilet. Maybe it was like the woman said, I needed something on my stomach.

A *tap-tap-tap* on the door and the woman asked if I was okay. When I said I was, she left me alone, and man oh man, I'm telling you, I was fucking alone. All I'd been doing was trying to find Nancy Noel—and look what I'd gotten myself into.

What bull! This was nothing more than the whining of a child who knows she's gone too far and wants her parents to bail her out. But ol' Mom was MIA, Daddy had drowned, and I was all by myself in some place where a courtyard held a reflecting pool, and stretching as far as the eye could see, miles and miles of sand.

I put my face in the bowl again.

The tears wouldn't stop. It was a crying jag like no other. All I could think was that I wished I'd taken Dad's advice and called Chad Rivers and asked him to take me dancing. I've never been bopped over the head while dancing. And it appeared that I never would.

Play at grown-up games and look where it got you. That was the problem: I didn't know what the game was. Or where I was. Maybe it was time to find out.

Half an hour later there was a knock on the door. I was slipping into a bra and underpants that fit—I didn't want to think about how they knew my size—then a pair of black cotton trousers gathered at the ankles, and a loose, maroon-colored blouse that covered my arms and came up to my neck. There were sandals for my feet and a scarf to cover my head. I left both in the bathroom. The delicious smell of breakfast overwhelmed the moist air when I opened the bathroom door.

"Mr. Faisal will join you as soon as you have eaten."

"Have him join me for a cup of coffee," I said, hoping she didn't see my trembling hands. I went over to one of the stools and sat down at the serving window.

"Oh, no. That would not be proper. In my country the women do not eat with the men."

"And what country would that be?" I asked from where I was lacing up my running shoes.

But she only smiled and returned to the other side of the window, through which she passed my plate. As I ate, I watched her move. The woman had a petite figure, and the body veil did not hamper her as she moved around the kitchen.

"Do you always wear that thing—what's your name anyway?"

"My name is 'Nadia.'" The woman glanced at the body veil. "I do not usually wear this, but you are new to this house and its customs. Usually I wear a dress. Sometimes, I even wear the kind of clothing you wear. I assume you find the *chador* offensive."

"Only to my feminism."

"Miss Chase, in my country there is no sharp edge to that word."

After another bite of egg, I said, "American women are known to be on the cutting edge of what it really means to be a woman."

"But what is it that you American women are searching for?"

"Equality." I didn't know where that came from. I'd never been much of a feminist.

"But that can only be found in a false environment, so in that regard your goal is a false god."

"Don't you mean 'goal?'"

The woman shook her head. "Not at all." As she cleaned the stainless steel sink, she continued, "Miss Chase, do you know what shocks an Arab person the most when they visit your country?"

I shook my head. The steak and eggs were damn good, but the most promising thing was that I'd been given a knife to cut my meat. Now the instrument sat across the corner of my plate. Soon I'd have it, or one of its relatives, down the cuff of my long-sleeved blouse. I pretended to busy myself cutting up the rest of my steak. I noticed a silverware holder in the drawer on the other side of the window—filled with steak knives.

"What is it that shocks an Arab person when they visit my country?" I asked, playing along.

"That you Americans worship at a variety of altars."

"We have what's called 'freedom of religion.'" And to me that meant the freedom *not* to attend church. Maybe that's why I'd been sentenced to this purgatory.

The woman shook her head as she washed and dried the skillet used to cook my eggs. "I am not speaking about the various denominations, but so many things are worshipped, despite the fact you have a commandment, handed down by your prophet, that you are not to set up any other gods above the One True God. But you do. Every American does this."

"I'm afraid I don't follow." I cut up the remaining steak. I wanted to finish with the knife and make it disappear, then have another appear on my plate.

Nadia came over to the counter, put down the skillet, and pushed the silverware drawer shut.

Rats.

"What I am saying is that it is shocking to learn an American might worship a car, their television, or their work. And though it is quite inappropriate, some of your countrymen appear to worship sex."

"But in your country, wherever that might be," I said with a smile, "you believe . . . ?"

"Religion is the center of our lives and—"

"Your religion condones kidnapping?"

When she turned away to wipe the stove, I reached across

the counter, fumbled for the drawer, and got it open. Seconds later I had another knife in the cuff of my sleeve. Now with the steel toes of my running shoes, I was ready for anything.

The woman was saying, ". . . will have to ask Mr. Faisal, but I do not think he has kidnapped you, Miss Chase. He has saved you from a rather worthless life."

"I'd like to be the judge of whether my life is worthless or not."

She faced me again, cloth in her hand. "Really? Are you sure you know your own mind? From what Mr. Faisal tells me, you, too, are searching."

"But the answers I found would be *my* answers." When I rested my arm on the edge of the counter I could feel the blade of the steak knife.

"And if they are the wrong answers?"

"They would still be my answers."

"And it would not distress you—all the time you had wasted by not utilizing the proper guidance?"

"I have plenty of people telling me what to do with my life, lady."

"I would recommend you heed the advice of Mr. Faisal— when he takes time to speak to you."

I gestured at the stylishly decorated room. "That's what this is all about—Mr. Faisal kidnaps women and then turns their lives around."

"You waste so many lives in your country . . . ."

"I'm not wasting my life," I said, losing my patience with this dumb bitch who'd obviously never read the Declaration of Independence. Neither had I, but every American knows about "life, liberty, and the pursuit of happiness." "Nadia, in my country it is permissible to waste one's life on whatever one wishes—cars, televisions, even sex."

"But it is still a waste," she said returning the eggs to the refrigerator.

"And your relationship to Mr. Faisal, Nadia?"

"I am one of his wives."

Steve Brown

"And that satisfies you, that you're one of many?"

"Miss Chase, the ways of your country are as strange to me as mine must seem to you."

"And about to get stranger." I took another bite of steak and eggs. "How many wives does Faisal have?"

"I think, Miss Chase, my husband would prefer to answer those questions."

"And when will I see him?"

"When you have finished your meal."

I pushed my plate off the window and into the sink where it hit hard enough to form a fault line. Nadia stared at the cracked plate as I took a last sip from my coffee.

"Then bring on the bastard. I'm finished with the appetizer and ready for the main course."

16

Mohammed Faisal turned out to be a short, stocky man, not the one who had hit me on the head with the flashlight back in Carolina. I shuddered. Back in Carolina. I had to maintain my focus.

Faisal wore a white linen suit, white shirt, and dark tie. His head was round and his black hair slicked back. He had a narrow mustache, his complexion was dark, and a small mole on the right side of his face sprouted several hairs. He gave me a polite smile and bowed slightly as he entered the room.

"Very nice to have you as a guest in my home, Miss Chase."

I was just waiting for the son of a bitch to get close enough to drop the knife out of my cuff and plant it in the middle of the jacket of that white linen suit. I could already see the blood and the stupid bastard's shocked look—when a huge man followed Faisal into the room and took up a position beside him.

You need another plan, Susan. The guy's bigger than two of you and you ain't no small thing yourself. The bodyguard was burly, dark, and lots of black hair. He wore a suit similar to Faisal's, stood way taller than me, and the mug was ugly. The bastard's nose had been broken in the past and not well repaired. He stared at me with small back eyes. A steak knife and steel-toed running shoes wouldn't make a dent in a guy this size.

Clearing my throat, I said, "You're a strange man, Faisal, happy when your guests wish they were somewhere else."

"Now, if you don't mind, Abdul will search you."

I gulped, then nodded my compliance. When the mug stepped toward me, I held my arms straight out as he ran his hands up and down my torso.

"Watch it, buster," I said, stepping away and raising my arms overhead so the knife slid toward my chest, hit there, and fell past my bosom.

The bodyguard took my arms and ran his hands up and down them, then did the same for my legs. Now the knife lay across my tummy. The ugly man ended his search and posted himself beside the chair. Throughout the search the bodyguard's expression never changed and his face stayed as ugly as it had been when the mug had first come through the door. He continued to stare at me with those small, expressionless back eyes.

"I imagine you have a great many questions."

I took a seat across from Faisal with the knife lying across my waist and hopefully hidden in the folds of my blouse. "Like where the hell am I?"

"Really, Miss Chase, you are going to have to do something about your language. Where you are going, that will not be permitted."

"There are a lot of things I do that are not permitted."

"That may have been true in the United States, but this is Saudi Arabia and a filthy mouth will not be tolerated by either a husband or a master."

"Then return me to the States."

Faisal shook his head. "That disappointing life is behind you. You have a new life. Here."

"And if I . . . and if I don't choose to stay?" I wondered how long I could put up this front without bursting into tears. My mouth had gone dry, absolutely no saliva to be found anywhere. My tongue frantically searched the inside of my mouth. I didn't remember being this frightened, and I'd been in some very tight spots before.

"But where would you go? It is hundreds of miles to the nearest city. No, Miss Chase, you must reconcile yourself that, in a house such as this, this is where you will spend the rest of your life."

"Is this what happened to Kathy Gierek, Agatha Mitchem, Jennifer Frank, and my friend Nancy Noel?"

"Some of those young ladies are in my country."

I looked at the bodyguard again. Nadia had made herself scarce. "Those girls must've been more taken with your accommodations because I can't say I'm impressed."

Faisal chuckled. "Besides the tongue, you also have a sharp mind. But you will learn, in my country, if a woman is smarter than her master, she would be smart to keep it to herself."

"The night you had me abducted, I'd just told my dearest friend I didn't think I was ready for marriage. Are you telling me you flew me all the way here for me to tell you the same thing?"

"Oh, no, Miss Chase. No one I know would marry a person such as you. You will become a concubine and I will receive a half million dollars as my fee. You are, as they say in your country, signed, sealed, and delivered."

"Signed and sealed, but not delivered," I gestured at the room, "unless this is my delivery point."

Faisal laughed. "I have no use for whores. It is my friends who wish to acquire them."

I felt myself tremble and it wasn't just from rage. The bastard seemed to have all the answers. Forcing myself to lean back in my chair, I said, "It sounds like you've got quite a racket."

"I have several commercial dealings in your country. My planes fly in and out of the United States each week. You were simply part of the latest cargo. I have agents along your East Coast, in Myrtle Beach and Fort Lauderdale. We once operated in New York City, but it turned out to be a poor return on the investment."

A nervous laugh escaped my mouth. "Snatching girls off the street and selling them for a fat markup—what possible overhead could there be?"

"Disease and drugs, not to mention there is more than one person working around the New York City Port Authority. Pimps and ropers abound. Myrtle Beach and the coast of Florida are much less competitive. And by the time those girls were processed, the waste was enormous."

"Meaning the ones you didn't keep, you knocked over the head and left in some dark alley."

Faisal shook his head sadly. "They would not have long to live in any event."

I shivered and rubbed my arms with my hands in an effort to warm myself. The knife lying across my belly was no consolation. It felt as cold as the rest of the environment.

"But you, Miss Chase, are quite healthy and will have many years with your new master."

"And when I'm old and gray? You haven't explained the retirement plan."

"I doubt you will ever see a gray hair in that blond hair of yours, which I never want cut again. Do you understand? I expect your hair to be much longer when I turn you over to your buyer."

"And if I shave my head the moment you leave?"

Faisal glanced at his bodyguard. "Then you will spend a night with Abdul, as has happened in the past to others who have disobeyed me. Whores amuse Abdul much more than they do me."

"Oh, the procurer doesn't sample the wares, slicing off a piece here and there?"

"I never deal with whores, Miss Chase."

"Faisal, where do you get this impression I'm some kind of streetwalker? Who's been talking out of school?"

"A young woman who lives alone and invites men to spend the night with her after flaunting her body at the beach—what are people to think?"

Leaning forward, I said, "I don't care what the hell you think, but I'm no whore."

"Miss Chase, I have asked you to not use such language in my home. Now stop it."

"Well, fuck you, too, and the camel you rode in on." I sat back in my seat.

The asshole spoke to his bodyguard in their native tongue and the ugly man crossed the room to where I sat. Involuntarily, I cowed, but the slap still found my face. The blow stung and brought tears to my eyes.

"You . . . fucking bastard."

When his master spoke to him again, Abdul slapped me again and I stopped cursing. Matter of fact, I stopped speaking. I was too busy sobbing, my face in my hands as the tears began to pour. "You—you have no right to do this to me . . . I'm an American citizen."

"You, Miss Chase, now have no rights at all. You are my property and I will deal with you as I wish. You are to be sold to one of my buyers as soon as your hair has grown out. Your hair will earn over a hundred thousand dollars, so you shall remain here until it grows out. And that tan of yours. You will not be allowed outside during the daylight hours. White skin is what your buyer is paying for and what he shall receive."

I wiped the tears away and looked up. Abdul had returned to his post. His eyes revealed nothing. The bodyguard didn't appear to care one way or the other, unless perhaps Faisal gave him the opportunity to spend the night with me.

"Where . . . where is Nancy?"

"Miss Noel is quite happy with her new master. She is treated royally, although I was surprised her buyer would pay full price since her brain had been damaged by drugs. I have to say that was a miscalculation on my part and now I would like to have more dull young women to sell. They make excellent concubines if they don't eat too much."

A boy stuck his head through the door and stared at me. He was a small, slender child, with black hair and eyes, and a dark complexion. He wore a brown short-sleeved shirt and black slacks. The boy stood where Faisal and Abdul couldn't see him, but something in my face gave him away.

Faisal's head whipped around. He saw the boy, said something in Arabic, and the kid disappeared, closing the door behind him. "That is my son, Miss Chase. My only son. All my wives have been quite disappointing in that regard."

"Will your bodyguard slap me for reminding you that it is the male of our species who determines the sex of the child?"

"Not at all. Abdul does not speak your language. It would damage too much property if my bodyguard understood how disrespectful you were being."

"Calling us 'property' is your way of desensitizing yourself to what you have done to these young women?"

"What I will also do with you, Miss Chase."

Jeez. This asshole never backed down. "You really think you're hot stuff, don't you?"

"Miss Chase, I have been doing this for a good number of years and have never had any difficulties. Why would things be any different with you?"

I smiled at the bodyguard and said, "Personally, I think you are lower than whale dung and this time you have picked on the wrong gal."

My master returned the smile. "You are what Americans call a 'quick study.' I admire the way you bend my rules to suit you. But you must remember that your intelligence and cleverness are not relevant unless applied to pleasing your master. What makes a woman safe in her home is that her husband, or master in your case, is pleased."

"And if I don't please?"

"Kathy Gierek already wears one scar. Another scar and her master might not think she is worth having."

I laughed when I wanted to cry. "Damage . . . a half-a-million-dollar . . . piece of goods." It was hard to get my breath. "Now that doesn't . . . make sense."

"I think he forgot he wore a ring when he slapped her, and of course, there was a delay in flying in a doctor to repair her face. But Miss Gierek will not raise her voice to her master again."

His story reminded me of how much my face ached. "This is how you like your women—submissive?"

"This is how women should treat their husbands—with respect. And the husband is obligated to provide for them."

"But the poor concubine . . . ?"

Faisal dismissed me with a wave of his hand. "That is a question of property and one in which I an not involved. Women will give me whatever I want when I am abroad and, in my opinion, that is where this business belongs."

"Was that a pun?"

"What?" He smiled. "Oh, I see—abroad." His face lost its smile. "Perhaps it is best for you to spend some time here, not only to let your hair grow out, but to give Nadia a chance to teach you our ways."

"Will I be able to see Nancy?"

"That has been discussed. There is a good deal of melancholy among these girls who have been abruptly separated from their culture. Many of my buyers have asked if I could work out such a rendezvous."

"So you're thinking of having them over for a cookout—here, at your place? Maybe even some concubine swapping?"

"I have placed twelve young ladies. Perhaps you could all get together, in small numbers."

"In the middle of the desert with a bunch of Arabs—I'd think they'd prefer the company of camels."

"Miss Chase, I am not going to sit here and allow you to be disrespectful to me."

"And how was that disrespectful, Master? I simply told you what was on these girls' minds and how you could cure their homesickness."

He considered this. "You are correct, Miss Chase, but it has not been decided."

Steve Brown

"You'd damn well better decide, because if I know these girls, they long for home, just as anyone would. You've probably had one suicide, maybe more."

"You know, I may have to break my rule about having my own concubine and keep you for myself. This is one of the more stimulating discussions I have had."

"And give up a half million dollars? Why, Mr. Faisal, I'm flattered you would even consider the idea."

Faisal stood. "I have spent quite enough time with you. Nadia will begin your education in a few days."

"What's wrong with her?"

"What do you mean?"

"I just wondered what about her made you feel she was safe with me, that she wouldn't be contaminated by my Western vices."

Faisal glanced at the kitchenette, then headed for the door.

My words followed him. "You don't think anyone will come looking for these girls?"

At the door, he faced me. "You should know that better than anyone. Agatha Mitchem was sold into slavery by her father before I found her, your friend, Nancy Noel, will never be missed now that you are gone, and Miss Gierek simply gave up on her boyfriend and the strike."

"And me?"

"Oh, Miss Chase, people on the fringe of any society are never missed. At first some of your friends will miss you, then they will wait for your body to turn up—which it never will—and finally they'll forget about you."

An icy knife of fear cut through me, but I was still able to get out, "Jennifer Frank's mother offered me money to find her."

"Then her mother will be disappointed. Jennifer Frank was one of the young women who is no longer with us—in this world."

17

After Faisal and his bodyguard left, I stared out the glass corner of the house, but I couldn't see desert. I didn't see myself in Arabia. I could only see miles and miles of ocean. A boy and girl were out there, riding a catamaran, side by side, and leaning back to get the best angle for traversing the waves. For once I was letting someone else steer. Well, what did you expect? It was our first date.

The boy was Chad Rivers. His wet hair hung over his forehead like a mop and he wore a pair of red bathing trunks. Water glistened on his tanned body; his shoulders were the type a girl could call home. There was plenty of definition in those arms as he worked the lines of the boat. Chad had narrow hips, a nice set of buns, and his strong legs strained against the side of the catamaran as we crashed through another wave.

I couldn't help but share his laughter as we soared down the coast to a secluded spot where he brought the boat ashore. We gathered firewood, built a fire, and laid a metal grill across several rocks over the fire. When the fire was only a pile of coals, the steaks were put on. Before that we lay on a blanket, drank beer, and made out. Chad kept working his tongue into my mouth and that made me tingle to my toes. Hands on my breasts, my nipples hard, top of my bikini off, I was enjoying this as much as he was—until he tried to pull off my pants.

"Please, Chad . . . ." I scooted away, working out of his arms. "I—I'm not ready for that."

He was not pleased. There was an intensity in his eyes and the thing between his legs was as big as a flashlight . . . like the one that had hit me over the head. That's why I was sitting here and staring over these miles and miles of sand. If Dads could only see me now.

More than once we'd taken Harry's schooner down the Intracoastal. Dads would sail and I would lounge in the stern with a line in the water, trolling for dinner.

"What's Chad's father working on these days?"

"Trying to build a better cigarette boat." Meaning those narrow, shallow-shaped boats with a slot for the rich to rocket up and down the coast in, leaving their shore-bound fellows green with envy. When you saw one, you just had to have it. Few did.

Dads took the pipe from his mouth. "Why's that?"

"The demand's made it worthwhile to manufacture." I tugged on the line. Still no bite, but there was plenty of time for that, plenty of afternoon to enjoy, plenty of life to enjoy. I lay back with my eyes closed, the sun frying me. It was one of the rare times I wore a bikini. "The Boomers have entered their cash cow years and have plenty of disposable income for speedboats."

"Interesting," Dads said, segueing to what was really on his mind. "Do you see much of him these days?"

Playing dumb, I asked, "His father?"

"No, Susan, the son."

"Every once in a while."

"Then I take it your relationship's not serious?"

"As serious as any." There really hadn't been many, but, hey, a gal has to keep up her image.

"I think he's one of the special ones."

"Dads, you've never come down one way or the other about any guy. You stay enthusiastically neutral."

"Because most of your dates are summer romances. How many young men hit on you while you're in that lifeguard stand?"

"Usually I blow them off."

"Well, I'd think twice before I blew off Chad Rivers." Dads realized how close he'd come to something a gentleman didn't want to say. His face turned beet red and I had little trouble with him the remainder of the day.

As often as not Peanut was along, and the memory reminded me of why I was stuck in Saudi Arabia. The dysfunctional looking for the dysfunctional, and see what you got. Tears ran down my cheeks. I didn't wipe them away.

Nadia was here. I hadn't heard her come in. "Anything I can get for you, Miss Chase?"

"A one-way ticket home."

"Actually, I only deal in the possible."

I sat up, planting my feet on the floor and feeling the cold steel of the steak knife across my tummy. "And what would you do if I killed you where you stand. What would Faisal do? Would he punish me severely to make up for the loss of one of his wives, and by doing that, blow off a potential half a million dollars?"

"Would you kill me, Susan?"

Oh, now we were chums all around. "No," I said, returning my attention to the miles and miles of sand. "But I will not be sold."

"And those feelings are why my husband wishes for you to return to your room so you can deal with your disappointment."

"And rage."

"Why is that?" She appeared genuinely puzzled. "You have lost nothing but the life you led."

I felt my eyes narrow. "What did your husband tell you about me?"

"That you were a whore. Not that I'm passing judgment, but what kind of life can that be?"

"Do you believe everything your husband tells you?"

"He is my husband," she said, looking at the floor, "and I honor him as such."

"Even if he's a liar?" I didn't add the obvious: That her husband was a kidnapper, too.

Nadia straightened up. "Susan, are you ready to return to your room?"

I nodded. I had some planning to do. Or a shitpot full of grieving.

For hours that became days, I lay on my bed going through what therapists call stages of grief. And why not? Susan Chase didn't exist and the steak knife didn't seem to be my one-way ticket home. How in the world would I get close enough to use it? Still, that didn't keep me from scheming. Problem was I couldn't fulfill any of my fantasies if I didn't have the lay of the land. I'd have to earn the right to move around. That glass corner in the living room had told me nothing, only depressed the hell out of me! My mind alternated between anger and rage, frustration and grief.

In the past I'd played cat and mouse. Most of the time I was the cat; now I was the mouse. While playing that game, you find all sorts of things to think about: putting together a dream team; or remembering stories having particular significance in your life, such as *Huckleberry Finn* or *The Outsiders;* or reviewing the high points of your very short life. One of those high points would be Harry Poinsett, who had made it possible for me to hold onto my boat after my father had fallen overboard and drowned.

The night Daddy disappeared and I dispatched the pirates to their watery graves, I had leaped aboard their boat, flipped on all their lights, and dropped anchor. Not that the anchor would reach bottom, but it would hold the boat in position long enough for me to try to find Daddy. It also gave Daddy a chance to find me. So with a bullhorn, and I might add a rather hysterical voice, I searched several square miles before the sun came up and the pirates' boat disappeared over the horizon.

Unable to keep my head up, arms trembling with exhaustion, voice gone, I returned to a marina where I moored *Daddy's Girl*—and fell into the arms of Harry Poinsett. Dads had brought his schooner around to pick up friends staying along the coast. In a whisper, and with Harry holding me on my feet, I told him what had happened. Harry only told the Coast Guard my father was drunk when he fell overboard.

I woke up in the hospital and found Harry asleep in the chair beside me. I couldn't raise him with my voice, so I reached over and shook him.

He sat up. "How you feeling, Princess?"

"Daddy?" I squeaked.

Harry shook his head. "Still no sign. His body might wash ashore later."

"But that can't be." Tears formed in my eyes. With Mama gone and my brother and sister dead, I'd be all alone. It wasn't fair, not fair at all, and here Harry Poinsett was calling me "Princess." Princess of what?

Dads took my hand. "There are people who want to buy *Daddy's Girl,* if you want to sell her. I can help you with that. The money could be put away for your future."

I shook my head. "I'll wait for Daddy. He'll be back."

Now Harry did more than hold my hand. He gripped it. "Susan, you must be realistic. Your father's not coming home. It's been over seventy-two hours—"

"Seventy-two hours?" I squeaked, sitting up. "Three whole days?"

"Yes, my dear." Harry kept patting my hand. "And the Coast Guard has found nothing"—his voice dropped and became conspiratorial—"but that other boat and one of the men who died . . . by your hand—they found that."

I gripped his hand tightly. "Did you tell?"

"Of course not. The Coast Guard may make the connection or they may not. There's been quite a bit of grass coming ashore around here. One thing you must get through your head is that your father's not coming home."

"Yes, he is!" I squeaked. "He'd never leave me."

From there our conversation went downhill, and the nurse had to give me something for hysteria. The following day the conversation drifted along in the same vein. And Daddy was still missing. It was Day Four.

"Susan, I don't think the authorities are going to let any fourteen-year-old girl—"

"I just turned fifteen."

"Oh, yes, I remember," he said with a grin. "All that screaming, hollering, and leaping off the pier. I didn't think you knew that many boys. As I said, Princess, I don't think the authorities will allow a girl your age to do anything without adult supervision."

And he was right. The Department of Social Services had been notified and a big, fat black woman was sent to see me. She, too, asked the same question: "Do you have any relatives, and if so, where do they live?"

There was an uncle in Florida, but Social Services wouldn't let me go live with him. He was recovering from falling off a high wire and was hospitalized himself.

"He's an acrobat, Dads, and in a full body cast. Can you take custody of me?"

"Susan, I don't think I'm the parenting type."

You can see how bogus that was after all the time Harry Poinsett has spent educating me. "But I want to be here if Mama or Daddy comes home."

"Then accept a foster home."

"I will, if we can work out a deal that you take care of *Daddy's Girl.* I have some money—I mean, Daddy had some. I can tell you where he kept it and you could take care of the boat until I'm on my own at sixteen." Sweet Jesus, but that seemed an awfully long way off.

"How do you know you can trust me? Remember, I'm the guy who's always telling you to turn down your music."

"I have to trust someone." Taking his hand, I said, "I'm begging you, Harry. I can support myself once I turn sixteen. It shouldn't be all that hard."

> *Ah, foolish youth,*
> *how little you know,*
> *how little you understand.*
> *But there's someone always to teach you,*
> *and we call that person The Man.*

When Dads agreed to take care of my boat, I joined my foster parents long enough to learn I would be their scullery maid—and be groped by my father when the foster mother's back was turned. The night the bastard came to my bed I grabbed him by the balls and didn't let go. His screams brought my foster mother running. Seeing her husband bent over, she asked him what was going on.

My foster father said, with tears in his eyes, that he'd been walking past my door when I'd asked him to come into my bedroom and then I'd come on to him. I tried to make my foster mother understand what a pervert her husband was.

My foster father called me a liar, and once he could stand, gave me the back of his hand. Nobody had ever hit me, not even Daddy. And if my new mother thought I had a filthy mouth, she had to wash out her ears with soap before going to bed. She said she'd call social services the following morning and have me put in another home. That didn't sound like any improvement, so I packed a bag and was gone before the sun came up. Very much like Agatha Mitchem.

By the time they found me, I was in Florida where I'd joined my uncle and the circus. He was happy to see me, as he needed someone to step and fetch it while wearing a full body cast. I didn't return to South Carolina until I was sixteen. After that, the state had no say whatsoever in what I did with my life. But now another jerk thought he could do just that—in frigging Saudi Arabia.

Let's suppose that what Faisal said was true, that I was being held hundreds of miles from the nearest city. I had no reason to doubt him and sooner or later I would get a glimpse of my surroundings. Hell, I'd already gotten a hundred and forty degrees out of a glass corner! I should keep my eyes open for how people came and went—in a place hundreds of miles from town and how a western woman could pass for an Arab. The *chador* might help, and in that, Nadia would be a willing teacher. I'd be as submissive as possible—even if it turned my stomach—and pick up as much Arabic as I could, not to mention the lay of the land.

The following morning, my education began and soon Nadia and I fell into a routine. After breakfast we studied the *Koran*, then we adjourned to the gym before a light lunch. It appeared Faisal wanted all of his "whores" in good shape, and in this regard I supported him one hundred percent.

Nadia was surprised at what I could do with Faisal's equipment. "I guess this is the first time one of your husband's whores has been in this good a shape, right?"

The woman said nothing, only stared at the floor. I learned girls were taught from birth to do that—when anyone challenged them. I went on with my workout, waiting for her to look up. "I'd expect most of those girls can't hold a candle to what I can do. Do you know why?"

Now she looked at me.

"Because I was never a whore. Whores live the life of a concubine in my country, too." That was a stretch, but this girl didn't have to know about the hookers working the Strip. I came out of the straps where I'd been curling my legs in a midair crunch and took a break on a machine that works your calves. "I was a lifeguard. My part-time job was looking for runaways. You know, kids who run away from home and end up at the beach. We get a good number of runaways, and since I'm close to their age, I can hang with them until I find who I'm looking for."

"Hang?"

I explained what that meant. God, this was killing me to be so positive and upbeat, but I wanted out of this place and maybe this stupid bitch would help me. At least not get in my way when I was ready to leave.

"I was useful to people, Nadia, not some whore. Even a few of the cops respected me," I said, remembering Lt. Warden.

I wondered if Warden was looking for me or had Harry told him I'd turn up eventually with a lame excuse for worrying everyone to death. Tears came to my eyes and I had to turn away from this woman who had no clue what it meant to be free and responsible for your life, and your mistakes. Warden had to be looking for me. I had to believe that. I had to believe in something.

"So one day this little boy came to me and asked me to find his mother." Using a towel to wipe the sweat away, as well as the tears, I told the story about Nancy Noel and how drugs had destroyed her mind, but that she had redeemed herself by supporting herself and her son.

"Yes," said Nadia, nodding. She no longer wore the body veil, but the same clothes as I. "I know her. She was here several weeks ago."

"She was?" I stopped wiping the sweat away and forgot about my tears. "Where is she?"

"She has a new life, Susan, as you will have one day."

"And does Nancy miss her son?"

"I—I don't know."

Little by little I broke her down. It seemed that Nadia was also an outsider. She lived well, but she also harbored a secret. What'd you expect? Two gals together, and unless you loved to study the *Koran*, there was little to do around this frigging place, though I was becoming a pretty good cook. People just had to hold their noses. The stuff these camel jockeys ate . . . and I had to eat it, too. No more steak and eggs. And there was no TV or radio. Hell, I'd even read the frigging newspaper if there'd been one. I did miss *General Hospital*, but strangely enough, not my cigarettes or liquor.

I was showing Nadia how to set the dip machine so you

rid yourself of most of your weight; in other words, how to do pull-ups without having to pull up your whole body weight. Nadia had never been able to figure how to max out the machine. When she used it, the shelf on which you knelt slammed up and down as it met its upper and lower limits. Now, with a little bit of help, she moved up and down with the grace and ease of a practiced performer. It appeared there were some shortcomings in the universal education offered by The Kingdom.

"I will miss you when you are gone." A sheen of perspiration covered the dark-skinned woman's face.

"Well, I can't stay forever." It'd been two weeks and I had the marks on my wall to prove it.

"I am truly sorry this has happened to you."

"Then you believe me?" I asked, my hopes soaring.

Nadia nodded. "At first I did not, but now I understand it is possible that my husband is mistaken."

I took her hand. "Then you'll speak to him?"

She pulled· away. "I cannot go against my husband's wishes."

"Even when it means I'll spend my life as a sex slave?"

"Susan, after all you have studied, you must see that a woman cannot go against her husband's wishes."

"Even when he kidnaps people and sells them?"

"Susan, please. A little over fifty years ago Saudi men bought and sold slaves openly."

"Fifty years ago. In the twentieth century?"

She nodded. "From tribes raiding across the border. And they were not slaves as you understand from your American Civil War. It was more like in Roman times when slaves were treated as part of the family. I grew up with slaves. They were my playmates, and little difference was shown between them and myself; more was shown between boys and girls."

"Funny, but I don't remember seeing this on the Discovery Channel."

Nadia had to be told what the Discovery Channel was.

Color Me Gone

"You must understand that what you are asking me to do is not only to go against the wishes of my husband, but also my culture. I cannot change what will happen to you."

"But why do your men treat you like this?"

"Susan, my people are desert people and a very savage race. Up until the time I just spoke of we were still raiding our neighbors, roaming the desert, slaughtering each other. Nowadays there is nothing for our men to do, nothing to occupy their time, nothing to challenge them. Certainly there are policies to be developed and accounts to be kept, but how can adding and subtracting sums of money turn a boy into a man, a boy who has been raised on tales of our violent and bloody history? Experiences he will never share."

"What does this have to do with the way your husband treats you?"

"When the international community came to Arabia, they came for the oil and there were certain things my people, especially the men, had to give up. They had to stop their violence. They had to stop dealing in slaves. Westerners showed our men how to be rich, but you failed to teach them what to do with their free time and how to obtain the proper status. Nowhere in the *Koran* does it say I am to be kept as a prisoner in my own home, that I cannot be seen on the streets, or that I am a second-class citizen. This custom developed rather quickly when our men were left with little to do, little to be respected for in the new society."

Nadia took a seat on the bench press. "Susan, would you believe at one time Saudi women fought beside their men against warring tribes? Those women knew they were important to their men. Now we provide a different importance by living behind the veil, staying indoors, and following our husbands' rules and restrictions."

"But why do you go along with this? Other women must know what you know, about your past and how important Arabian women have been to The Kingdom."

"But where would that leave our husbands?"

"Maybe it's time the jerks grew up."

She smiled. "I think I will be long in my grave before that happens and much sooner if I were to press such claims."

"Are you saying he'd kill you? I can believe all this about the status of women, how it evolved, and how a husband only has to say three times that he divorces you, and presto, you're gone. But to actually kill you, that I can't believe."

"He would kill me," she said firmly.

"Once again I have to ask to what advantage?"

"Why do you think I am the one who trains you, the only one you ever see?"

"I have no idea, Nadia. I supposed this was your house— like you told me, each Saudi husband has a house for each wife. This one was built for you."

"Oh, it is, but I never go anywhere. I am always here."

"Not even into town? Why?"

"Because it would shame my husband for me to be seen in public."

"Shame him? Why is that?" I looked her over and the loose fitting clothes she worked out in. Despite the sags and bags of the fabric you could tell this woman had a decent figure. "You're an attractive woman, Nadia. You could never be an embarrassment to any man."

She stared at the floor. "I am barren, and without children I have no status. This means I am of little importance. For this reason I am very happy to be included in my husband's scheme, despite how low it makes me appear in your eyes. Without my husband I am nothing."

"That's why Faisal trusts you?"

When she looked up her eyes were wet. "He knows I do not wish to be cast out or returned to my family."

"How did he explain your disappearance to your family?"

"Susan, when I left my father's house I ceased to exist—if my husband so chose. And he so chooses."

"You're a nonperson in your own country?"

Nadia smiled tolerantly. "Most Arab women are such nonpersons, while other simply live more interesting lives."

For some reason the gym was the only place Nadia would

open up and talk. Perhaps the gym was the only room in the house that wasn't bugged. Later, as I became more familiar with Saudi culture, I realized that no male would have any interest in what any wife, child, or concubine might say, even if plotting against him. And the way my hair was growing and my tan disappearing, I was very interested in putting together some sort of escape plan. But would Nadia help?

"Is it like Faisal says, that I am hundreds of miles from the nearest city?"

Nadia nodded.

"Is there any transportation, a car, a truck, a jeep?"

She shook her head. "My husband arrives by helicopter."

"But I've never heard a chopper arrive."

"The room in which you stay is soundproofed, and that is where you remain whenever he arrives."

"So this place was built for running a white slavery ring and you were brought in to tame the girls."

"Here I can be of service to my husband."

"Is Faisal here now?"

Nadia shook her head.

"How many others are here?"

"There is only you and I and the desert surrounding this house." She took my hand. "You must put these ideas from your mind. There is no escape—for you or me."

I returned her grip. "Why don't you leave with me? You can get asylum in my country."

She let go of my hand. "Susan, you shall never see your home again. You must accept that or you will go crazy."

I tried to ignore the chill sweeping through my body. "Why . . . why do you say that?"

"Because that young woman you continue to ask about— the one my husband said was cut with her master's ring. It was my husband's ring that cut her. Kathy Gierek was here less than a week and tried to escape twice. The second time my husband had her put to death. And he made me watch so I could relate her story to those such as yourself."

18

Two weeks later a helicopter arrived, bringing my master and my new destiny. Since I'd been missing for over three weeks, I had to hope that Dads, Lt. Warden, or Chad—someone—was looking for me. Looking everywhere, that is, but in frigging Saudi Arabia.

Nadia took me to the "men's" side of the building where Faisal and a greasy-looking fellow waited in the tent room. Many of the Arab royal houses, and a few of the homes of bigwigs, have rooms decorated like tents, like in silent movies where Rudolf Valentino seduced any number of women. It's supposed to pay homage to their desert roots, or where their grandpas may have seduced any number of women.

A fabric-draped ceiling forms a circle in the tent room; in a few places the drapery hangs to the floor and in other places it is tied firmly to the side, giving the illusion that the fabric could be brought down to complete four walls of a tent. It's all for show, except where the overstuffed pillows are piled against the back wall. The area in front of the seated master is where the serious business takes place, and heaven help the person who does not kowtow to her master.

The supplicant must stand or kneel before the semicircle of pillows. These pillows are the Arabian version of overstuffed chairs with no arms or legs. Armrests are provided by long circular pillows, and throw pillows are placed here and there for the master's comfort. A pillow or two might be provided for the supplicant to kneel on or sit on at a table while she offers her master a drink.

The bodyguard, Abdul, stood to the right of Faisal and Faisal's son, and my buyer sat on the other side of Faisal. The greaser's name was "Aziz," and he was distantly related to the founder of The Kingdom, as these a-holes like to call their frigging sandbox. Aziz wore a long white gown with the traditional headdress and black band around the forehead, and sandals on his feet.

Faisal wore his usual business suit. In fact, I'd never seen Faisal when he wasn't wearing a suit, but Abdul always wore traditional Arab garb. The ugly-looking bastard didn't seem pleased since I hadn't given him any reason to spend the night with me. And I wouldn't. I'd hold my tongue until I got a shot at getting out of this damn place. I was under no illusions that there would be only one chance at escape. For that reason, I told myself over and over again that there was nothing these bastards could do to piss me off. Well, that's what I thought.

The greaser who was buying me had dark features, a mustache, goatee, and long fingers covered with thick black hair, and his teeth were in need of some serious dental work. The man's face lit up when I walked into the room. So did Faisal's son's. As much as I'd prepared myself, their reaction took me by surprise. I don't usually have that kind of effect on men, or else they're much better at concealing it.

Over a breakfast I didn't touch, Nadia had told me about what the morning held. "My husband has asked if you will embarrass him. If you do, you will certainly pay a price, but nothing compared to what I will pay. My husband cannot take his anger out on you, more than allowing Abdul to spend the night with you. From what I have learned during the time we have spent together, I think it would distress you considerably. When your friend Kathy Gierek was here and she rebelled against my husband's authority, my husband took the lash to *me.*"

"You're kidding?" I don't know why I was surprised. A little tense, I guess. Just a little.

She stared at the floor again. I was getting pretty sick and tired of this no eye-to-eye contact. "Susan, I am not saying you must concern yourself with my situation, but I would not care to feel that lash again."

Nadia pulled up the back of her blouse and turned around where I could see where a bra strap ran across scars from the lashing. I shook uncontrollably, jerked down the blouse, and tucked the hem into her belt. Nadia said nothing and I didn't know what to say.

As we sat there, a peace gradually came over me. I realized I no longer feared Faisal, or Abdul, because I was a dead woman. Faisal had said there was little chance I'd ever escape from here, or from the life he had planned for me. He might be right, but I would not be anyone's prisoner.

"Pull the hem of your dress above your knees, Miss Chase," ordered Faisal.

I took a deep breath and told myself that I was ready for this. Still, it took a long time to pull up my dress. The only person in the room it didn't affect was Nadia. On second thought, as I watched the poor fool staring at the floor, I saw a tear start down her cheek.

All other eyes were on my legs. As I have said, I never wanted to be part of any strip show, but here I was making men's blood boil, and one little boy's. From his seat beside his father, the kid stared at me with eager dark eyes. What did this teach him about his relationship with women?

"Turn around, Miss Chase."

I did, slowly turning around. When I faced those eyes again, they gazed on me as if I was the entrance to Paradise.

"Very well," Faisal said. "You may drop the hem."

Color Me Gone

Aziz leaned over and said something to Faisal.

My master nodded. "Take off your blouse."

Though I'd been preparing myself for this, when it came to the moment of truth, I had trouble with the buttons. My head felt like it was about to burst and my ears roared. The room disappeared in a red mist.

Out of the mist, Faisal said, "Help her with the task, Nadia, and when we are through here, you and I will discuss why Miss Chase is wearing running shoes instead of sandals."

Refusing to wipe the tears from my eyes, I stood rigid. Three men and a boy were about to get a look at my boobs. Lollie Lloyd had been right. I didn't have the nerve to take my clothes off in public.

"Remain calm, Susan, and everything will be fine."

"Fine by whose standards—yours or theirs?"

Nadia smiled—I could see that much—then unbuttoned the front of my blouse. I had been told not to wear a bra. At that very moment, she stood between me and the men, dabbing my eyes with the ends of my blouse. Her compassion helped me regain my composure.

"Sometimes they are nervous . . ." was all I heard from Faisal, then, "You will be well served."

Nadia moved out of the way and I was totally exposed. And they say blondes have more fun. Perhaps they do, but only in a society where those bimbos can ride on feminist coattails.

"Remove the blouse, Miss Chase."

I gulped a deep breath—nearly hyperventilating—then remembered to breathe slowly and . . . pulled back my blouse, stripping for all eyes to see, shoulders held back so they would see me in all my glory. Again I shuddered.

"Please turn around," said a voice from out of the mist. "And take off the blouse."

My eyes burned, tears pooled up in my eyes, but the opportunity to turn my back on these bastards motivated me to shuffle around. When my back was to them, I could finally collect my thoughts. I would not give in to my rage—or humiliation. No. I would not. Nadia smiled reassuringly. It didn't help. Three weeks with the bitch and I hadn't been able to turn her. But neither had she been able to change my mind—no matter how many times we bowed toward Mecca.

Something was said in Arabic, probably commenting on my ass or the fact I was losing my tan. In English, Faisal said, "You have done good work staying fit, Miss Chase."

"But my hair is still too short," I said, turning around and pulling on my blouse.

"I did not give permission for you to cover yourself."

I continued to button up my blouse.

"Miss Chase, you have done quite well so far. Continue to do as I ask."

"Why? I've already been sold." Then in Arabic, I added, "I cannot respect or obey any man who makes love to goats and creates such a hideous child." I inclined my head in the direction of Faisal's son before spreading my feet and finishing my blouse.

I'm sure Nadia's eyes grew wide with horror. Perhaps even her mouth fell open. She had taught me how to say "making love to goats," never knowing those words would be used against her husband. Faisal's son looked at his father. He knew those words, but for them to come from the mouth of a woman . . . .

Faisal spoke sharply to Abdul and the ugly-looking mug moved in for the kill. When he was only a few feet away, I looked at the floor in a gesture of submission, then brought up my foot into his groin, thus recruiting another voice for the Vienna Boys' Choir. I might be missing my gaffs, but the steel toes were still there. Abdul screamed and bent over as I fumbled in the waist of my dress and brought out the steak knife.

Holding the bodyguard's head while he was bent over, I plunged the blade into the side of his neck. "That's for Kathy Gierek, you son of a bitch!"

The knife found an artery and spewed blood. The big man

was dead moments after hitting the white-carpeted floor. Next were Faisal and the greaser who thought he could own me. I advanced on them, both men in shock and still sitting on their cushions. My appearance did little to comfort them: knife in my hand and blood running down my arms.

Sell me like a piece of meat! I'd show them!

Both men recoiled against their armless cushions.

"Stand up, Faisal, and drop your drawers. I'm going to fix you so you can sing soprano."

Faisal's son was the first to react. He leaped off the cushions and ran out of the tent room. The other two could only sit there and stare. Probably the first time they'd seen the dark side of the Force—feminism, that is.

Faisal cleared this throat. "Miss Chase . . . ."

"Stand up, you goat lover."

The greaser who'd wanted to own me put his hands along his sides and tried to push himself up. As he did I brought my foot up, kicking him under the chin. The blow lifted him off his feet and knocked him into the wall of the make-believe tent. He rolled over, one side of his face caved in. Blood ran from his mouth.

Out of the corner of my eye, I saw Faisal reach for the knife. I swung at him. The blade sliced into his jacket, then his arm. Faisal fell back, screamed, and grabbed his arm. These guys weren't so tough after all.

Something hit me over the back of the head. I saw stars, my legs weakened, and the knife fell from my hand. I turned around to see pieces of a vase falling from Nadia's hands. Then the blackness closed in on me.

19

I woke up with the worst headache. I looked around. I was in a dimly lit room and lay face down on a bed with only a bare mattress. There was nothing in the room but the bed, and on it I lay naked. Instinctively, I felt between my legs.

No soreness. Nor was there anything running down my legs. I touched where I'd been hit over the head and winced. Tears came to my eyes. It took quite an effort, but I sat up.

Sitting on the side of the bed, I slid my hands between my thighs and shivered. The small room was air conditioned, and when I moved my feet, one of them hit something. I bent over to investigate and the movement nearly caused me to toss my cookies.

A plastic baggie filled with ice lay on the floor. I picked it up gingerly and placed the improvised ice pack against the back of my head. I sat there and tried to figure out what the hell had happened and who had stripped me naked? Most importantly, who'd hit me over the head? Better yet, where the hell was I?

I'd been arguing with Dads over whether to marry Chad

Rivers . . . and left in a huff and taken a walk to cool off . . . when some bastard had hit me over the back of the head with a fucking flashlight!

And the son of a bitch had stripped me naked and stashed me here until he decided it was time for fun and games. So this was what had happened to Nancy. But what good did knowing do me? I had to get out of this place and in a hurry.

A voice came from the ceiling. A woman's. "Susan? Are you awake?"

I twisted around, trying to locate the sound but only felt the pain in the back of my head. Better to remain still.

"Susan?" came the voice again.

But why would a woman lock me up? I couldn't make sense of it and I didn't recognize the voice. I remembered a strange dream about women . . . from some scene in the *Arabian Nights,* stripping for horny bastards at the Open Blouse.

"Susan," came the voice again.

"Yes . . . yes?"

"How do you feel?"

"What the hell do you mean 'how do I feel?' I was clobbered over the back of the head, stripped naked, and dumped in here." Pain racked my head and made me nauseous. There would be no more screaming.

"I'm sorry I had to do that."

You had to do that. What the hell was going on? Why would a woman hit me over the head and strip me naked? "Where are my clothes?"

"My husband thought it best you not have any clothing. You might have another weapon."

This was a husband and wife team? "Well, I'm freezing my ass off in here."

"Susan, I thought we were friends . . . ."

"And we'll be friends again when my clothing is returned."

"That is quite impossible. You are to be put to death this afternoon."

"Put to death!" I came to my feet, forgetting all about my

head and my stomach. "What the hell are you talking about? Who the hell are you and what right do you have to kill me? Is this what you did with Nancy Noel?"

"Susan, are you all right?"

"I'm sitting here in the darkness, naked as a jay bird, the back of my head cracked open, and you have the nerve to ask me if I'm all right. You bring your ass in here and I'll show you all right."

There was a long pause before she asked, "Susan, do you not recognize my voice?"

"Not only do I not recognize your fucking voice, I don't know where I am."

There was a long silence before she got back to me. But I wasn't waiting. I was padding around, trying to find a spot where I could get a point of leverage. I'd tear down these fucking walls . . . .

Kill me this afternoon! Uh-huh. I'd better come up with something and be quick about it.

I ran both hands over the walls, finding a glass window with chicken wire or something in it, then the seam of the door. But there was no knob. I kicked it, then yelped and hopped over to the bed where I fitted the ice pack to my foot.

Shit!

The woman was saying something.

"What?"

"I will speak to my husband. I do not think he would want you to die unless you knew what it was for."

I laughed. "Shit, lady, neither would I."

And the voice was gone, leaving me to rage at my helplessness, and nakedness.

A few minutes later, the door opened and a woman in peasant garb and a man in business clothes—with his arm bandaged—stepped into the room. In the man's good hand was a pistol, in the woman's another baggie filled with ice. I covered my breasts and my crotch, but had the feeling that being naked was the least of my worries.

"Who are you?" asked the man. He had the same accent—like the guy who had hit me over the head.

"You don't know who you're about to put to death? What kind of pervert are you?"

He pointed the pistol at my face. "Tell me who you are or I will shoot."

"Since you're going to kill me anyway, what difference does it make?"

"Miss Chase, I mean what I say."

"So, after you kill me, will you drop me in some sinkhole in the swamp?"

"Swamp? There are no swamps in my country." He looked at the woman, unsure of what to do.

"See," said the woman. "I told you it would do little good to kill her. She has no memory of the shame and humiliation she has caused you." The woman glanced at his injured arm. "Or the wound she inflicted on you."

I glanced at the injured arm held across the man's chest. I'd done that? Well, chalk one up for the home team.

"It's a trick," said the man. "You are trying to trick me."

"It's not a trick, you sorry fuck," I said, picking up the ice pack and advancing on him, "and if you put that gun down, I'll rip off your other arm."

Involuntarily, he stepped back. "I have a pistol, Miss Chase."

I continued to advance on him. "But you're not a natural lefty, are you?"

"But I will shoot you," said the man, backing toward the door.

"You couldn't shoot anyone," I said, continuing toward him. "You haven't got the balls."

The woman gasped, then stepped between me and the pistol. "Susan, watch what you say, please."

"This lousy bastard can only kill me once and I'm sick and tired of being pushed around."

Hiding behind the woman's skirt, the man said, "I was to have your head chopped off, but now I will drown you by my own hand in the pool in the courtyard."

The pool rang a bell. Something about miles and miles of desert behind a retaining wall . . . but that couldn't be along the Grand Strand.

"Please leave, husband. I will prepare her for her death."

"Fuck that!"

I threw the baggie over her shoulder. The little bastard ducked and I leaped at him. The movement knocked the woman into him and the gun went off. I slapped the weapon away and kicked him in the groin—before remembering I wore no shoes. I yelped, but so did he. When he went down, I snatched up the pistol and limped out of the room, down a narrow corridor toward a light. I had to shield my eyes as I entered a room that appeared to be on the second story of the building. My eyes couldn't help but be drawn to a glass corner overlooking a courtyard with a small pool, then, behind a stone wall, miles of sand.

To say I was stunned would be an understatement. I fumbled my way to the glass corner, then put my hands against the glass to make sure it was real. Below me was the courtyard with its pool and palms, then miles and miles of sand. It appeared I had stumbled through the Stargate.

Turning around, I took in the room with its modern furnishings, the kitchenette, and a pair of doors to God knows where.

Where the hell was I? The bastard with the crushed set of balls would certainly know. Returning to the room where I'd been held prisoner, I found the woman dead—the bullet had entered her back and ripped apart her heart—and her husband lying on the floor holding the family jewels. In light from the hallway, I kicked his injured arm and he screamed.

• "Where the hell am I?"

The asshole rolled away, moaning as he went.

I followed him and kicked him again. "You son of a bitch!" I think I was becoming slightly unhinged. "Tell me or you're not going to have any arm left."

The asshole noticed the dead woman lying beside him.

"What has happened here? What has happened to Nadia?"

"You killed her, that's what happened."

"No! You must have done it!"

I stuck the pistol in his face, and the son of a bitch scooted away until he ran into the wall. "If you don't tell me where I am, I'm going to have my own Operation Desert Storm."

Once he told me, I couldn't believe it. Forgotten was any thought of being naked. "Are you serious?"

He nodded.

"But why, for God's sake?"

"Because you are a blonde, Miss Chase." He righted himself, leaning against the wall, the injured arm lying across his lap. "My people will pay a good deal of money for blondes."

"And that's what happened to Nancy Noel?"

He nodded, then stood up, using his good hand on the wall and grimacing in pain. He brushed down his pants with his good hand. "Now, Miss Chase, if you will, give me the pistol."

I leveled the weapon at him. "And why would I do that?"

"Because there is no way you can escape. Tourists are not allowed in The Kingdom, certainly not females traveling alone. Anywhere you should go, members of the Public Morality Committee would find you and turn you over to the authorities." He glanced at Nadia lying in her own blood. "For killing my wife."

"Fuck you. I'm getting the hell out of here."

"And how is that, Miss Chase?"

"I'm thinking about it. I'm thinking about it." But in truth I had no idea. "What's your name, asshole?"

"Faisal."

"Shit, Faisal, you've got to have a car, a truck, or something . . . ?"

He shook his head. "There are no vehicles. No roads in or out. As I told you before, you are hundreds of miles from civilization."

The bastard spoke with such confidence he might be telling the truth. Still, I didn't believe him until I'd put on some

Steve Brown

clothes and made a thorough investigation of the place. The son of a bitch was right. There was, however, a helicopter pad and that meant I could leave—if I used my head.

The two of us stood in the dry, blistering heat, staring at the pad with the "X" painted on it. "Call in a chopper."

"Certainly, Miss Chase."

As we returned to the compound, a small hand came down from behind the stone wall and knocked the pistol away. It was a damn kid, but I only hesitated for a second before spinning around on one foot and putting the side of my other foot against the boy's head. The little twerp went down in a heap and started crying. Daddy was scrambling for the gun, but when I put a steel-tipped boot up Faisal's ass, he screamed and went sprawling—across the pistol. Faisal was bringing up the weapon when I threw a kick at the pistol, missed, and hit his wounded arm. Faisal screamed and the pistol fell from his hand.

I went over and picked up the gun. "Frigging amateurs."

The kid was crying and holding the side of his head. Daddy said something in Arabic from where he lay.

"Shut up! I don't understand the lingo and I don't want to hear it."

"I was only telling the boy that everything is going to be all right."

"Everything's not going to be all right. His mother's dead and you think you're going to kill me."

The boy wiped his tears away. "You struck my father. You will pay for your insolence."

I couldn't help but laugh. "I kicked you—will I pay for that?"

"You will!"

I looked from the boy to his dad and back to the boy again. "I know you think women are second-class citizens, but damn, kid, I'm the one holding the gun."

"You will not be holding it much longer." He used his hands to stand. "And then you will be put to death." He brushed off his shirt and pants. "Possibly by my own hand, if it pleases my father."

Jeez. Were there Sammy Noels everywhere in the frigging world?

He walked over to stand with his father who had gotten to his feet. "We will see you in your grave."

"I've taken about all this I can stand." With the pistol, I motioned them into the building. "Time to call that chopper. And, Faisal, I'll shoot the boy in the kneecap if you do anything funny."

"I understand."

We went back inside and through a room that thought it was a tent, a room like in those silent movies where Rudolf Valentino seduced any number of women. A red stain on the floor looked like blood.

Behind the tent's fabric wall was a door. Faisal took out a key and opened it. Inside was an oak desk and matching cabinet with a couple of chairs. On the desk were photographs I didn't remember being taken of me. I also noticed my lack of a tan and the length of my hair.

"How long have I been here?" I asked as Faisal went around to the far side of the desk.

"Almost a month. You were to be sold this morning, but you upset my buyer."

"That sounds like me. Now call in the helicopter." I pulled his son over. The boy didn't want to come, but when I slapped him, he decided to cooperate. "Put that on my tab, kid, if you get the chance to off me."

The boy did not smile but neither did he cry.

"You wouldn't kill a boy, would you?" Faisal held a cell phone.

"I damn well would and consider it a blow for feminism." Gesturing with the pistol, I said, "Speak English or your son dies, and for some reason I think you'd consider that a greater loss than your dead wife."

"It would be. Wives can be replaced, sons cannot."

"Then you'd best remember that." I jammed the pistol against the boy's head. "One word in Arabic, or whatever the hell you speak, and the boy's history."

Faisal nodded, then made the call. "I am ready to leave," he said into the phone. A pause and he added, "Only my son and me. No one else." He broke the connection. "They should be here in a half-hour."

I nodded, still holding his son. "And no tricks."

"Why should there be? You cannot escape."

I locked them in the room where I'd woken up, but first I had Faisal drag his wife out. Locking up the kid with his dead mother might be a bit much. After that I returned to Faisal's office where I used the phone and called home. I got Dads. It sounded like I woke him up.

"Where are you, my dear? I've been out of my mind with worry."

"Do you have anything there to drink?"

"Anything . . . to drink? What in the world do you mean, Susan? Where are you?"

"I'm being held prisoner in Saudi Arabia."

"Saudi Arabia? I thought you were looking for Nancy Noel."

"She's here. I just haven't found her. I need a little time."

"I don't understand . . . ."

"White slavery, Dads, that's what I'm talking about. I was abducted the night you and I fought over whether I should marry Chad Rivers or not. When I went for a walk to cool off, some guy hit me over the head and kidnapped me."

"Susan, I'm having a hard time believing this. The Saudis are very good friends of ours, very good friends of mine."

"Dads, I really don't have time to argue the point. Just promise me you won't call any of your friends over here. But you can call Chad and tell him I've missed him."

"All right, Susan. What is it you want me to do?"

Send lawyers, guns, and money. Instead I told Harry to contact the American Embassy and tell them a blond-headed gal was on her way in, that she was an American citizen, and she'd be seeking sanctuary. Then I went out to meet Faisal's helicopter.

20

There were four of them, dark-looking guys with square shoulders and square faces and dressed in desert fatigues. They dropped off the chopper before it landed, hit the ground, and rolled to their feet. They came running toward the compound—which was as far as they got.

While waiting for the chopper, I had jury-rigged a couple of leaking gas tanks to both sides of the door, so when the commandos came through, I put a bullet through the closest tank and they were toast. It almost cost me the helicopter.

Since the doorway was blocked by men engulfed in flames, I jammed the pistol into my belt and ran for a palm tree tilted to the side, one practically paralleling the wall. I ran up the length of the tree and flung myself in the air. I landed with a thump and was lucky that the top of the wall hadn't been salted with broken glass. But hey, why would you do that when you were out in the middle of the frigging desert?

Landing on the wall jarred my teeth and took my breath away. Shit. Jackie Chan makes this look so easy. The sound of the chopper revving its engines got me moving. I pulled myself up and over until I lay across the top of the stone

172

wall. Then I swung down the far side, losing my grip, landing on my back and jarring my spine.

The helicopter was a Huey-type with open bays, and it slowly lifted off as I got to my hands and feet. Stumbling toward it, I realized this wasn't going to cut it. I gritted my teeth and ran, actually loped, then leaped for the landing gear as the chopper brought its nose around. The pilot tried to flick the skid away, or hit me, whatever. He missed, but I didn't.

I got both arms around the skid and hung on as he lifted off—over flames which were his buddies. I pulled my body over the rounded piece of metal, grabbed a strut, then got a hand on the open deck—when the chopper suddenly turned on its side. My hand slipped off the deck and I found myself hanging on the skid by one arm. Pain burned in my shoulder and I had to concentrate on bringing my free hand around and grabbing the skid, then wrapping both hands around it. That didn't make my shoulder feel any better.

Catching my breath, I saw an oasis ahead of us. As we approached the cluster of trees, the pilot leveled out and headed for the palms. Arabs wearing traditional black robes and watering their mounts stared as we flew toward them. Mouths fell open. A gal hanging from the landing gear of a chopper wasn't a sight you often saw in this part of the world.

Fifty yards away from the oasis I lifted my feet, then my legs and hips onto the skid, forcing the pilot to circle around and come back for another try. It appeared he was willing to chance it just to get rid of little ol' me.

The Arabs on the ground tried to control their frightened animals. They waved and screamed and one of them took a shot at us as we came in the second time. I got a hand in the bay, then one on the open hatch and pulled myself inside. Leaves from the palms slapped my foot as I pulled myself onboard. That might've been when I wet my pants. Or first noticed they were damp.

The pilot saw me on my hands and knees in the bay and rolled the chopper to one side. I grabbed the webbing on the bulkhead and hung on tight. Still, I went headfirst out the open bay, followed by my feet. The desert leaped into my face. I didn't know how much more of this I could take.

Pulling myself straight up and into the bay by its webbing, I grabbed the frame, feeling the ache in my arms, my back, both hands scraped and bloody. When the pilot looked again, I forced a little smile.

He cursed and threw a fist in my direction. I laughed hysterically, then sobbed into my shoulder and held on tight. Finally, when he leveled out, I was able to climb forward— toward the seats.

He shoved me back as I pulled out the pistol. The blow caused me to stumble back and land in the web seat against the rear of the bay. After catching my breath, I went forward and stuck the pistol in his ear. He was trying to turn the helicopter on its side.

"Straighten . . . out." Tilted to one side, I was trying to keep my shoes from slipping out from under me.

Once the chopper leveled out, I held the pistol where the pilot couldn't reach it and scanned the horizon. Nothing but miles and miles of sand. If Faisal's kid was any barometer of what men thought of women, turning myself into the authorities wouldn't help.

I was considering my predicament when we passed over an oil rig. I motioned at the rig with the gun. The pilot glanced at it and shook his head. I popped him upside the head and in no time we were kicking up sand on a landing pad owned by British Petroleum.

I wanted an American rig and shouted that into the ear of the first man who ran over, a lanky fellow with thinning hair. In his hand was a clipboard, in his shirt pocket a plastic protector filled with pencils and pens.

"Yes?" he screamed, leaning into the chopper.

"Looking for an American rig."

He pointed to my left. "To the east about five kilometers."

"Tell him," I said, motioning at the pilot with the pistol.

The English guy saw the pistol, realized the front of my

blouse was covered with blood, and drew back.

"Tell him!" I shouted, pointing the pistol at the Englishman now.

He told him in Arabic, then backed away, and we were off again, sailing across more miles and miles of sand.

It was an Exxon rig, and I was polite enough not to mention that they were part of a conspiracy to run up the price of gasoline along the Grand Strand each summer. We landed and kicked up sand again.

People on the rig stopped and stared. Another lanky young man ran to the pad, holding onto his hard hat. He wore a long-sleeved shirt with the sleeves rolled up, jeans, boots, and a pair of designer sunglasses. As we yelled at each other, more men walked over and stared at the chopper, whose blades continued to raise sand.

"Know where the American Embassy is?" I hollered. The pistol was held between my legs where he couldn't see it.

"It's in the capital."

"Would you recognize it from the air?"

"I think so. What's the problem?"

I showed him the pistol.

He stepped back. "What's this?"

"Get in!" This episode was testing the limits of my nerves. I didn't know how much longer I could last before I shot someone out of sheer frustration.

The young man climbed in as I slid out of the way and gestured him into one of the seats. The pilot shook his head and muttered something about Allah. The poor fool probably wasn't used to women taking charge of his miserable life. Others moved toward the chopper as its blades continued to whirl. When they saw the pistol, they backed away; a horn blared over the noise of the chopper.

"How far is the capital from here?" I screamed in the ear of the engineer as he buckled in.

"Two hundred or so miles."

"Can we make it on the fuel we have?"

The guy checked the fuel gauge. "No way."

I flashed him my remaining smile. "Well then, fill her up!"

Men hustled out of a mobile home with shotguns in their hands. They ran in our direction.

"And tell those guys to get lost. I've already killed four men today. You don't want to be the fifth."

"Just who the hell are you, lady?"

"Susan Chase. I'm a lifeguard from Myrtle Beach."

21

Dads and I were sitting in deck chairs on the stern of his schooner, sharing drinks with Peanut and his mother. Me and Nancy enjoying our beers, Dads and Peanut were drinking soft drinks. It was a beautiful August day along the Waterway. Hot, sunny, and not a cloud in the sky. Speedboats pulled skiers behind them, cruise boats paddled downstream, and absolutely no sand was in sight. Since returning to the States I hadn't been near the beach.

My boss was not pleased with my taking off, and I tried to convince him that it hadn't been of my own accord. Marvin wasn't persuaded. He muttered something about my taking a vacation during the Season.

Nancy looked fine, but disappointed me by saying, "You know, Susan, I didn't mind being over there." She glanced at her son. Peanut had his feet hooked under the railing a little ways down and was staring across the Waterway. "Oh, I don't mean that I didn't miss Sammy, but those people take real good care of you."

Peanut got to his feet, and left the boat.

"They treated me like royalty. A young girl took care of

me, and I had all sorts of exotic clothes; things you wouldn't consider wearing unless you worked at the Open Blouse. Which I have to do again, if I want any money."

"But you had to screw that guy, that prince, anytime he wanted."

"Well, yes, but I was treated like a real princess."

Which is what any girl *thinks* she wants and Nancy was still a girl at heart. It appeared her prince had fed her well, fattening her up for the fuck, you might say, because she had an extra roll peering over her shorts.

"Nancy." Dads was watching Peanut kick a rock into the pines down the road from the marina. "I think you need to spend more time with young Samuel. It won't be long before he returns to school and you won't see him again until the holidays."

Nancy stared down the road where I'd gotten bopped over the head. Even in the heat Peanut wore charcoal gray slacks, tan penny loafers, and a white-on-white shirt with sleeves rolled up. Hands plunged into his pockets, shoulders hunched over as he walked along.

"He wants to be alone. I've seen him like that before."

"And the next time you see it, you should ask him to go out for an ice cream."

Nancy didn't understand.

"Dads means Sammy wants to spend time with his mother but doesn't know how to ask."

"He may not even know it, Nancy," added Harry.

"I don't think so. I embarrass him."

"It doesn't take much brainpower to love someone."

Harry flashed me a sharp look. "Go be with your son, my dear. He may not like it, but he'll know you care about him and that's what really matters."

Nancy looked at me, and when I nodded, she got to her feet, stepped off the boat, and walked down the dock after her son in the fancy clothes. Me—I wore cut-offs and a cropped top and was exposing myself to the sun again—and to any guy who might come along. Right now it would have to be a special kind of guy. One who didn't mind all the bandages, the cracked ribs, and a separated shoulder.

When Peanut realized his mother was following him, he picked up his pace. Nancy looked at us and Harry threw her an encouraging wave. She ran after the boy, whooping it up. With a look of horror, Sammy ran down the road, his mother chasing after him.

"That's not going to work, Harry."

"Never go to your grave not having loved enough."

"Then that leaves me out of the equation."

"Then you haven't known many men."

"But you can't say I haven't tried."

"Susan!"

"Just kidding, Dads, but I can tell I was missed."

"Everyone missed you, Princess."

"Because—like Warden said—I'm a pain."

"I wouldn't put it that way."

"You were so mad that I'd stormed off your boat and not eaten dinner that you blew me off. It was a whole week before you realized I was missing. Am I that bad?"

"I filed a missing person's report."

"With Warden?" I asked, after sipping from my beer.

"He and DeShields were at some seminar in Columbia, something to do with the latest development in DNA fingerprinting. They didn't know you were missing until they returned."

I leaned over, winced as the pain hit my shoulder, and patted his knee. "It was nice to be missed. By someone."

"My dear, you had me scared to death."

"I was scared to death. Spend the rest of my life as a concubine—I don't think so!"

"Some of the most influential women in history were concubines."

I harrumphed. "Nowadays guys marry our brains and get our bodies as a bonus."

"I'm sure that's something a girl as attractive as you likes to believe."

"Dads!" I said, sitting up. The pain in my ribs and shoulder made me sit back down. "You're no better than Faisal."

"And what became of Mister Faisal?"

"I understand he has lost considerable face and may have to move his operation overseas, the legitimate one, that is. Though I'm sure he'll be back in the white slavery business soon enough."

"Thanks to you, Faisal's name is on Interpol's list of known white slave traders."

I shrugged and the shoulder reminded me I shouldn't be doing that.

"And you were cleared of charges of killing his wife."

"Actually, the Embassy said if I left the country and never returned there wouldn't be any investigation."

"You don't look happy about that."

"It means Saudi women aren't even worth an investigation into how they died." Clearing my throat, I looked out over the Waterway. "I didn't kill Nadia, but when my memory returned, I realized she'd been as much of a friend as she could. The fact that her husband will go unpunished . . . ."

"Don't dwell on the negative, Princess. The girls you were looking for—how many did you locate besides Nancy?"

"I'm not sure I like being called 'Princess.' Kathy Gierek was killed trying to escape. Faisal had her beheaded, so I was lucky. I don't think I would've gotten a second chance. Everyone knows about my mouth."

"I'm surprised you survived the night, much less a whole month. Shows you have real potential for self-control, Prince—Susan."

"And once the Giereks finally believed me, they hired a lawyer to open negotiations to have her body returned—if they can locate the grave. They don't mark unknown female graves in that country, especially those of concubines. Jennifer Frank OD'd in the States and never made it to The Kingdom. Her body will turn up along the Grand Strand and the story won't be reported because it'll hurt the tourist trade."

"Susan, please."

"Aggie Mitchem decided to stay over there."

"You aren't pleased with her decision?"

"I thought she should come home."

"And work for Daryl Flaxx or someone like him?"

"She could do better."

"Which, when they see you on that lifeguard stand, people think the same of you."

I took a swallow from my beer. "Aggie has a home—until her Prince Charming tires of her. Then he'll have her head lopped off and her body buried in an unmarked grave. It'll be like she never existed."

"Perhaps she never did, Susan."

I sat there, thinking helpless thoughts, and determined not to go on a crying jag like I had the moment the helicopter touched down at the American Embassy and I fell into the arms of a Marine guard.

Harry said, "The strikers won their fight at the Open Blouse. You have to be happy about that."

"Flaxx agreed to provide health benefits for the dancers after they've worked ninety days. Pregnancy won't be covered."

"Half a loaf is better than none."

My face ached. I was about to start crying again. No way could I stop—until a black Corvette pulled into the parking lot and a handsome guy stepped out. He wore a blue-and-white pullover and a pair of jeans and waved at me from the car. The guy's hair was a mess. He'd been driving with the top down again.

I put down my beer and stood up, holding onto the railing to steady myself. Actually, Dads had to give me a hand. Concerned appeared on Chad's face as he walked down the pier toward Harry's schooner. That look was almost as precious as when he smiled that little smile meant only for me.

"Should I stay up?" asked Dads, watching me hobble down the gangway to meet the guy with the special smile.

"Not unless you want another long wait."

ABOUT THE AUTHOR

A member of the Mystery Writers of America and Sisters in Crime, STEVE BROWN is also the author of *Radio Secrets*, a novel of suspense about a radio psychotherapist with a secret past; *Black Fire*, the story of a modern-day Scarlett and Rhett facing a church-burning in South Georgia; *Woman Against Herself*, a suspense novel in which a single mom takes on a drug kingpin; and six novels in the Susan Chase Mysteries series.

Steve lives with his family in South Carolina. You can contact him through www.chicksprings.com.

COMING MAY 2004

COLOR ME GUILTY
A SUSAN CHASE MYSTERY

by Steve Brown
ISBN: 0-7434-8001-5

I was close to tears. This was my godchild who was missing. Hell, her grandparents didn't think Megan was missing. Like everyone else, they thought she was dead. But I knew better. I'd known from the moment that dirty diaper had been stuck in my face. Megan was alive!

I just needed to find a way to prove it...

In the third Susan Chase Mystery, lifeguard and runaway finder Susan Chase meets her match in a killer who leaves a string of clues—and a trail of dead kids who can tell no tales....

"With the potential to devlop a cult readership, it might be wise to pay attention to Susan Chase."—*Booklist*

ALSO AVAILABLE

COLOR HER DEAD
THE FIRST SUSAN CHASE MYSTERY

by Steve Brown
ISBN: 0-7434-7973-4

Color Her Dead introduces one of the most interesting, attitudinal, and sexy mystery heroines in years: Susan Chase, a lifeguard who moonlights as a runaway finder.

With cranky, penny-pinching Mrs. Rogers wants her 26-year-old daughter found, Susan almost refuses. To locate the missing woman, she must sort through a series of jealous lovers, artistic temperaments, drug pushers, lecherous art dealers, and spoiled rich boys.

She has the usual number of doors slammed in her face, and as she closes in on the location of the missing woman, Susan is thrown down a flight of stairs, assaulted on her houseboat, accused of trespassing—and of murder.

"Plenty of action accompanies this in-your-face, likeable heroine… a good selection for most collections."—*Library Journal*